SEASONS FOR CELEBRATION

A Contemporary Guide to the Joys,
Practices, and Traditions
of the Jewish Holidays

Rabbi Karen L. Fox
and
Phyllis Zimbler Miller

illustrations by Vicki Reikes Fox

A PERIGEE BOOK

Perigee Books
are published by
The Putnam Publishing Group
200 Madison Avenue
New York, NY 10016

Library of Congress Cataloging-in-Publication Data

Fox, Karen L.
Seasons for celebration : a contemporary guide to the joys,
practices, and traditions of the Jewish holidays / by Karen L. Fox
and Phyllis Zimbler Miller; illustrations by Vicki Reikes Fox.
p. cm.
Includes bibliographical references and index.
1. Fasts and feasts—Judaism. 2. Judaism—Customs and practices.
I. Miller, Phyllis Zimbler. II. Title.
BM690.F69   1992
296.4—dc20   92-7428 CIP

ISBN 0-399-51764-2

Cover design by Irving Freeman
Back cover photo © by Bill Aron

Book Design by Rhea Braunstein

Printed in the United States of America
6   7   8   9   10

This book is printed on acid-free paper.

To our parents—
Senta and Dave Fox
Ruth and Albert Zimbler

Our husbands—
Michael Rosen
Mitchell Miller

Our children—
Avi and Benjy Fox-Rosen
Rachel and Yael Miller

ACKNOWLEDGMENTS

We want to express our gratitude and appreciation to Vicki Reikes Fox, whose love of Judaism inspires her art. The illustrations within this book capture the beauty and meaning of significant Jewish moments.

We also wish to thank our agent Susan Zilber and agent Sandra Watt for all their support and enthusiasm. Many thanks as well to our editor, Laura Shepherd, who navigated this project to its successful conclusion.

Thanks to our friends and colleagues for their ongoing encouragement and assistance. And special thanks to our husbands for being there.

CONTENTS

INTRODUCTION

WELCOME! Although the two of us come from different childhood backgrounds, and even today from different viewpoints of Judaism, we share a love of celebrating the Jewish holidays with our families and friends.

We are fortunate that we have access to vast resources of communal Jewish life. But we also know that celebrating the Jewish holidays without support networks and without sufficient resources can be difficult and overwhelming. It can be especially challenging for those Jews who were brought up without much experience with Judaism and for those who have newly chosen to join the Jewish people.

On the other hand, we also know that becoming involved in celebrating Jewish holidays can be extremely satisfying for individuals and families. Celebrating the holidays throughout the seasons can provide a focus, an anchor that binds us to our past and future. This is especially true in today's frenetic world, where people find themselves isolated from reassuring experiences reminiscent of their childhoods.

We have written this book to assist those who want to know about the Jewish holidays. We've tried to explain both the basics and the more sophisticated concepts while providing very specific information on rituals and related activities. We also offer ideas to children and adults, individuals and families.

What makes our holiday book different from other available books? We hope that we have a unique perspective, neither so traditional nor so liberal, but one that provides the specifics of the holidays and then offers suggestions for augmenting those specifics. We've also kept in mind the myriad claims made on all our lives and tried to suggest ways to incorporate these holidays into one's own life-style. We believe that

Jewish holidays enhance life experiences and Jewish life experiences strengthen one's self-esteem and personal identity.

If we have been able to convey even a part of the joy of celebrating these holidays with family or friends and given you a place from which to start or continue, our efforts will have been well rewarded.

Hag Sameach—Happy Holidays to You!
Rabbi Karen L. Fox
Phyllis Zimbler Miller
Los Angeles, California
January 1992 / *Shvat* 5752

GUIDE TO USING THIS BOOK

*S*EASONS *for Celebration* has been divided into separate chapters for each major holiday to make this book easy to use.

The holiday description begins with a general introduction and an appropriate holiday greeting. "Home Traditions" are highlighted first, followed by "Synagogue Traditions."

"Insights" provide contemporary philosophical or theological discussions. "Activities" include art projects, intergenerational sharing, music and book recommendations, and practical resource information. "Recipes" offer traditional Jewish fare with a modern twist. The authors' personal anecdotes and experiences are interspersed throughout the text.

"Blessings" provide the most important prayers for the home traditions. The prayers can be used as they are presented in English and Hebrew transliteration and may be supplemented with a prayerbook that includes the Hebrew text.

All Hebrew or Yiddish words other than the main holiday names are set in italics when they appear for the *first* time in each chapter. The index gives page number references for these words. They are transliterated from the Hebrew alphabet into phonetic English spelling.

The Appendix explains the Jewish yearly calendar and lists Jewish holiday dates through the year 2005. The Appendix also offers a brief listing of the minor Jewish holidays not included in this book, as well as the addresses of selected Jewish organizations.

1
SHABBAT—A WEEKLY OASIS OF PEACE

IT has been said that more than the Jewish people have kept Shabbat, Shabbat has kept the Jewish people. Shabbat, the Sabbath, links us to the past, to all Jews who celebrated this weekly holiday in different countries at different times. Today, it ties us to Jews who speak a myriad of languages throughout the globe. It is a continuing Jewish link in time.

Shabbat, beginning each Friday evening at sunset and concluding Saturday evening at sundown, means different things to different people. For the most traditional in the Jewish community, it means the complete cessation of all ordinary work-related activities, such as driving, cooking, writing, building, buying, and selling. It is a day set aside to rest in specifically Jewish ways.

Others, more liberal in their definitions of work and rest, designate this weekly holiday by celebrating some of the traditions of home and synagogue observances, special meals, and also include social activities and unique recreational pastimes.

The origin of this holiday comes from Genesis, the first book of the Bible, in which God created the world in six days and rested on the seventh. In the Ten Commandments, found in the Book of Exodus, the fourth commandment is "to remember and to observe Shabbat, to keep it holy" (Exodus 20:8).

This statement—"remember Shabbat and keep it holy"—pinpoints the philosophical questions associated with Shabbat: What does it mean to remember a specific time each week? How is a sacred moment in time designated? What actions demonstrate that Shabbat is a Jewish day of rest? How are some everyday actions differentiated to denote Shabbat as sacred?

These theoretical questions lead to the practical ones that all Jews experience: How do we celebrate Shabbat? How do we distinguish between work and rest for Shabbat? How do we make Shabbat relaxing and rejuvenating?

The importance of Shabbat is twofold. Not only is Shabbat central to the preservation of the Jewish people, it is also important as the model of a Jewish holiday. The concepts of rest and work developed for Shabbat are applied to other Jewish holy days. The rituals for each holiday remain the same, using candles, wine, bread, and spices. The community-based celebrations of meals, worship, and social experiences are carried over from Shabbat to other Jewish holidays as well.

GREETINGS

The words used to greet one another on Shabbat are *"Shabbat Shalom."* When people say this, they wish their friends and family a "Sabbath day of peace."

HOME TRADITIONS

Jewish holidays start before sunset and end after sundown the following day. This means that Shabbat is welcomed on Friday evening and bid farewell to each week on Saturday evening.

Friday Evening

Observance of Shabbat begins, as do all major holidays, by reciting the blessing over the candles. The custom of lighting two candles comes from the dual-concept phrase "to remember and to observe" Shabbat.

While two candles is the minimum, some people light one candle for each person in the household. Candles can be set on a mantelpiece, on the Shabbat table, or another central location. A tradition is to allow the candles to burn out on their own—a glowing candelabrum adds beauty and warmth to the home.

The candlesticks can be ordinary ones or they can be special candlesticks used only for Shabbat. Various materials such as silver, brass, stone, ivory, or crystal can be used. Shapes can vary from ultrastark and modern to ornate traditional European varieties.

THE WANDERING CANDELABRUM

My grandmother Fannie (for whom I'm named) always lit all seven candles in her seven-branched Shabbat candelabrum: one each for herself and her husband, one for each of her four children, and one for her mother, of blessed memory. When my grandmother died at a young age, my grandfather gave away the candelabrum to a synagogue in a small Southern Indiana town near his home.

Years later, when the synagogue disbanded, the candelabrum was miraculously returned to a great-aunt of mine. She sent it on to my uncle and aunt.

My aunt kept it for several years until one day, unexpectedly, she sent it to me. She said at the time, "One never knows what will happen." A month later she learned she was dying of cancer. She had sent the candelabrum to me to ensure its place in our family.

When our children were born, I began to use the candelabrum in her honor—a woman who sincerely cared for the preservation of our heritage.

—P.Z.M.

As a home-centered ritual, candle lighting has traditionally been done by women, although men can also light candles. Some people recite the blessing all together; in other households only the person lighting the candles recites the blessing.

The kindling of light preparatory to the twenty-five hours of Shabbat separates the sacred Shabbat time from the workaday world. Some families who are not home by sunset light Shabbat candles just before they begin the Shabbat dinner. Shabbat candle lighting is the significant act that welcomes Shabbat into a Jewish home.

After candle lighting, it is customary for parents to bless their children, encouraging them to grow strong in the image of the biblical characters: Joseph's sons Ephraim and Menasshe for boys, or the matriarchs Sarah, Rebeccah, Rachel, and Leah for girls.

The Shabbat dinner is a festive meal. The table is set with a fine tablecloth and good dishes, silverware and glasses, and often fresh, seasonal flowers. As with many other Shabbat activities, this setting distinguishes the meal from the rest of the week's meals.

Everyone stands around the dinner table and begins with the singing of "Shalom Aleichem," the song that acknowledges the desire for Shabbat peace in every home. Some folks also sing "Shabbat Shalom," an upbeat, welcoming melody for Shabbat.

The ritual continues with the recitation of the *Kiddush,* the blessing over a full glass of wine (or grape juice). This is chanted with a melody that reflects the country in which one lives or from where one's family has come. In some homes the head of the household sings the Kiddush; in others, everyone chants the blessing together. Similarly, some households share one Kiddush cup, while others drink from individual cups.

The Kiddush declares the holiness of Shabbat. It highlights the dual thematic origins of Shabbat: God's rest after the creation of the world and the freedom experienced after Jewish liberation from Egyptian slavery.

Following Kiddush, an additional blessing is recited, this time over the *challah,* the special Shabbat twisted bread. Many families use two loaves of challah, symbolic of the double portion of *manna,* the "bread" miraculously given to the Jewish people for Shabbat while they wandered in the desert.

When reciting the blessing, some people hold two challahs together in the air, while others invite every person to touch the challahs that have been placed on the table. Some simply touch another person who's touching the challahs. One loaf is either cut or torn, depending on one's custom, and a piece is shared with everyone

at the table. Some households sprinkle salt over the challahs before distributing the pieces.

---------------------------------- ----------------------------------

O EXCUSE ME!

A specially decorated cloth is used to cover the two loaves of challah until after the Kiddush is recited. Why, you ask?

Tradition has it that the challah is covered so *that it will not be embarrassed when the wine is blessed first. After Kiddush, we uncover the challah and voilà! the challah alone becomes important in welcoming Shabbat.*

---------------------------------- ----------------------------------

The Shabbat evening meal should be one prepared with greater care than the weekday meals. Ashkenazic Jews—those from Russia, Poland, and other Eastern European countries—introduced the custom of serving chicken soup or gefilte fish for the first course, frequently followed by a chicken dish. Sephardic Jews—who come from Greece, Turkey, and other Middle Eastern countries—often serve spicy stuffed meats and rice dishes. Although it is traditional, chicken is not required for the Shabbat meal!

After dinner, it is time to sit back, enjoy the conversation, and sing a few Shabbat songs. We conclude by singing *Birkat Hamazon,* blessings of thanksgiving for the foods we have eaten, which can be found in Shabbat prayerbooks and songsters.

Saturday

On Saturday morning it is customary, after services, to serve a festive lunch. The meal begins with the blessings over the wine and challah. The meal is again followed by the singing of Birkat Hamazon.

Because traditionally no "work" is done on Shabbat, many people serve a cold lunch, while others have their own systems for keeping food hot. The *cholent* (recipe p. 25) of Eastern European heritage is a stew of meat and some form of carbohydrate (potatoes, rice, beans), which has cooked over a slow fire since before Shabbat began. Sephardic Jews have their own version of this called *adafina.*

Saturday afternoon is frequently a quiet time. Some folks cannot wait for their "Shabbat nap," while others enjoy visiting friends and engaging in special activities.

Concluding Shabbat

At the close of Shabbat, *Havdalah* is performed. This special home ceremony bids farewell to the day of rest, using wine, sweet-smelling spices, and a special twisted candle. The memory of Shabbat is savored by smelling the spices, warming our hands over the candle, and tasting the sweet wine.

The ritual is a short service, which is usually sung, and is found in Shabbat prayerbooks. All lights are turned off in the house; only the twisted candle glows.

The spices can be a combination of cinnamon, cloves, and nutmeg. They can be simply held together, pushed into an orange, or combined in a formal spice box. When camping, it is fun to use pine needles and other sweet-smelling plants for Havdalah.

As the candle is extinguished at the close of the ceremony, we hope that the Shabbat sweetness, found in the wine and the spices, adds to the richness of the week to come. Havdalah concludes with the hope that Shabbat peace will encourage peace for the whole world.

SYNAGOGUE TRADITIONS

Although the bulk of Shabbat liturgy follows the same pattern of prayers as weekday services, the Shabbat prayerbooks add special liturgy highlighting Shabbat values. Most synagogues have prayerbooks in Hebrew with English translations.

Evening

For the most traditional in the Jewish community, the men go to early Shabbat evening services prior to Shabbat dinner, then come home and enjoy a leisurely meal.

In modern times for many people it was often difficult to attend synagogue before dinner. Therefore, to encourage the awareness of Shabbat and to respond to those realities, many American synagogues in the late nineteenth century established the custom of late Friday evening services after dinner for everyone.

For Reform and Conservative synagogues this became the most popular Shabbat service. The innovation allowed the adults and children to celebrate Shabbat as a community and provided instruction through a sermon or discussion. Even today, this service encourages contact with the temple community even if one does not observe Shabbat throughout all of Saturday.

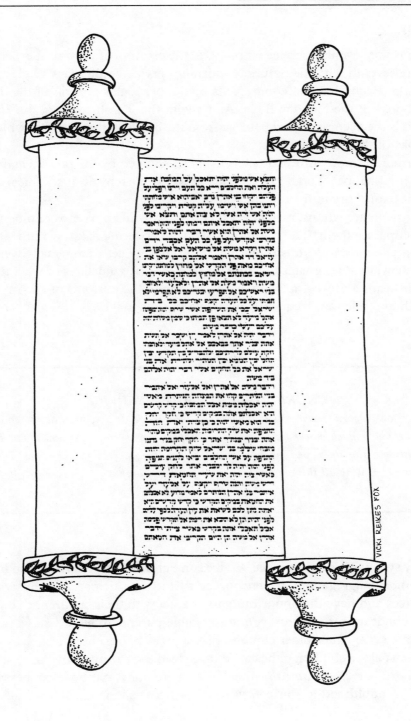

VICKI REIKES FOX

Morning

While the Friday evening service emphasizes the creation of the world in six days and rest on the seventh day, the Saturday morning service emphasizes God's revelation to the world. Each Shabbat, congregants read a particular portion of the *Torah*, the first five books of the Hebrew Bible. Along with the Torah reading, the *Haftarah* is sung. This is the accompanying passage from the books of the *Prophets*, which are the latter books of the Hebrew Bible.

A sermon or more informal talk is usually delivered by the rabbi. He or she may focus on the Shabbat Torah portion of the week, current events, ethical issues, or other topics appropriate for the congregation.

In most congregations, men cover their heads during prayer to remind them that God encompasses them. The traditional skullcap covering is known in Hebrew as a *kipah,* or a *yarmulke* in Yiddish. During Saturday services men usually wear a *tallit,* a unique shawl that designates the time for prayer. The guidelines of whether women cover their heads and wear a tallit vary according to the customs of each synagogue. Both kipah and tallit are frequently available in synagogues.

--------------------- ---------------------

CHOREOGRAPHY OF THE SERVICE

When you go to synagogue services, you might be surprised to see how much movement—bending, standing, sitting, rising up on one's toes—occurs in Jewish services. Why all this action?

We move as a community to emphasize the importance of certain prayers and to show respect to the Torah. Just follow along. Don't worry, you'll catch on!

--------------------- ---------------------

Many synagogues have special services on Saturday mornings for children, often called "junior congregation," to encourage them to participate. Parents can attend these services and have the opportunity to interact with their children. Some temples also have childcare for the very young to enable parents to attend services.

In some synagogues older children play a greater role in services than in others. It is not unusual for children to be called up to lead the closing song. Once a child has become a *Bar* or *Bat Mitzvah*—the Jewish ceremony symbolizing passage from childhood to adulthood at thirteen years old—he or she is considered an adult for purposes of participation in synagogue ritual. Some synagogues especially encourage the participation of teenagers, and consequently teenagers feel their importance within the temple.

The concluding Shabbat service, Havdalah, can be conducted at the synagogue as well as at home.

INSIGHTS

Why Shabbat?

In many places in the world, religion is no longer an integral part of our lives. For Jews, Shabbat has suffered from the prevalence of this belief, resulting in a splintering of the Jewish community and a loss of a personal weekly oasis.

Reclaiming Shabbat is a voluntary act, an act that affirms the value of a Jewish day of rest that is different than the typical notion of weekend.

In the *Shabbat Manual*, published by KTAV Publishing House, Inc. (New York, 1972) for the Central Conference of American Rabbis and edited by Rabbi Gunther Plaut, the purposes of Shabbat observances are treated in contemporary terms. These themes underline the significance of Shabbat for our lives:

Shabbat is a day that heightens awareness of the natural world. It offers an opportunity to meditate on one's own role in the natural setting and one's response to the seasons of the year.

Shabbat is a day committed to freedom. The Jewish people were liberated from Egyptian slavery, and they celebrate that exodus with each Shabbat. The pressures of the workaday, secular world are lifted, and Shabbat becomes an opportunity to set aside homework, housework, and professional obligations. It is also an opportunity to be freed from the drive for materialism.

Shabbat links the Jewish people, past and present, near and far. Jews use the same ancient rituals, perhaps in a new form, as their ancestors have done for generations. Shabbat also offers an opportunity to participate in a people with history, values, and future vision.

Shabbat strengthens personal lives. Through Shabbat rest, one can experience joy, contentment, and inner peace. Shabbat is a time to appreciate the special loving qualities of friendships and family.

Shabbat stresses commitment to peace. Peace in the world can be anticipated when peace is experienced at home. Jews do not try to change the world on Shabbat; rather, they experience the peace of Shabbat.

Definitions of Shabbat Rest

The basis of Shabbat as a day of rest comes from a biblical injunction:

> Six days shall you labor, and do all your work; but the seventh day is a
> Shabbat of complete rest, holy to the Lord Your God. On it you should do
> no manner of work (Exodus 20: 9–10).

Through the ages the definitions of work have always been a challenge. This original biblical source for Shabbat does not specify what kinds of work are forbidden. In other biblical citations certain types of work were prohibited: kindling a flame (Exodus 35:3); plowing, harvesting (Exodus 34:21); gathering wood (Numbers 15: 32); baking, cooking (Exodus 16:22); carrying (Jeremiah 17:22); and buying and selling (Nehemiah 13:15–17).

Even with all these additional citations, prohibitions against work were still unclear. The rabbis who later compiled and edited the *Talmud,* the largest code of Jewish law, listed thirty-nine major categories of work. In addition, they noted other activities not in the spirit of Shabbat rest.

Abstinence from work is a major expression of Shabbat observance, yet it is no simple matter to define work today. Some activities that one person does for work, others do only for relaxation or personal expression. In general, one should refrain from one's normal, earning-a-living activities and engage in that which is enjoyable and relaxing.

Many contemporary writers have attempted to define work and rest for today's Shabbat. In Rabbi Abraham Joshua Heschel's beautiful book *The Sabbath: Its Meaning for Modern Man* (Farrar, Strauss and Young, New York, 1951), the author states:

> Six days a week we wrestle with the world, wringing profit from the earth;
> on the Sabbath we especially care for the seed of eternity planted in the soul.
> The world has our hands, but our soul belongs to Someone Else. Six days
> a week we seek to dominate the world; on the seventh we try to dominate
> the self.

The essences of Shabbat are found in Heschel's thoughts. It is each Jew's challenge to find meaning in the customs and the enrichments of Shabbat life. How individuals define rest is less important than the fact that they choose to rest on the Shabbat day.

The four major American Jewish religious movements (Conservative, Orthodox, Reconstructionist, and Reform) have all interpreted and reinterpreted the notion of work and rest in light of their individual philosophical viewpoints and today's changing technology. You can study the various religious viewpoints and choose a Shabbat observance level that enhances your own life.

ACTIVITIES

1. Shabbat can be an opportunity to enhance family life:

a. Candle lighting is an important ritual by which Shabbat is welcomed into the home. Do it together even if the whole family will not be together throughout the evening. It connects you to each other and to Shabbat.

b. Shabbat dinner may be the opportunity to share the best and the worst of the week's experiences. Each person can share, be comforted, or congratulated. Try different ways to enhance your experiences with Shabbat dinner.

The phone can be taken off the hook (there's always the answering machine to take messages), and total concentration can be given to each individual at the table.

Find out what the children are learning in school, discuss current events, share the frustrations and challenges of adult life.

c. Children can be responsible for sharing a short story or an art project each week. After dinner is a good time for children to "show and tell."

d. Board games are a terrific Friday night or Shabbat afternoon activity. There's actually enough time on Shabbat to finish a complete game of Monopoly.

e. Reading stories together with young and older children brings closeness. Enjoy reading and discussing the stories.

f. Playing ball, walking, talking, and enjoying each other's company without the rush of having to be somewhere else are unique Shabbat opportunities.

g. Some families especially enjoy a chance to play in the park or bike throughout the neighborhood. Others visit museums or art galleries as a Shabbat activity.

Because Shabbat occurs weekly, it offers a regular place and time for family life. No matter how hectic the rest of the week is, you can look ahead and know there is a time that adults and children will have for each other.

2. These communal times can be enhanced by ritual items that are greeted each week as visual symbols of this special time:

a. Parents and children may enjoy doing art projects to create home ritual items such as challah covers, spice boxes, wine cups, challah plates, and candelabra.

Cloth for a challah cover can be cut from any type of appropriate material as long as it is large enough to cover the two loaves—it might be 15″ × 20″. Either fringe or hem the edges of the cloth.

The cloth can be decorated with realistic or abstract art. Young children can use fabric paint to create designs on the cover. Older children can draw with permanent markers, or glue appliqué designs on the fabric. Needlepoint or embroidery can be used to create designs of the challah itself, intertwined with representations from nature or flanked by the Shabbat candlesticks and wine in the Kiddush cup. Feel free to utilize the illustrations found within this book for decoration ideas.

Each week the challah cover is welcomed to the table. The "beauty" of the visitor adds to the specialness of the occasion. These treasures become precious heirlooms.

3. What other ways can you make time special? Rabbi Abraham J. Heschel noted that Shabbat is a "palace in time." He tried to convey the timelessness and beauty associated with Shabbat. Consider this concept and brainstorm ways that it can come alive for you and your household.

4. Shabbat is traditionally a time of hospitality. Some synagogues have a committee that arranges for visitors to have Friday evening dinner or Saturday lunch with a host. Frequently synagogues organize community Shabbat dinners or lunches for parents with young children, single adults, or newcomers to the temple.

But don't wait for an invitation. Do the inviting yourself and encourage people to share their Shabbat experiences in your home as well. Make a simple meal or do a potluck. Everyone will enjoy being together for Shabbat.

JEWISH HOSPITALITY AROUND THE WORLD

In August of 1979 on the island of Contadora, off the west coast of Panama, my husband and I had a surprising Shabbat hospitality experience.

When we had arrived at the resort hotel we found that our assigned room did not face the ocean. Mustering my courage, I asked for a room facing the ocean, and we were moved accordingly.

On Friday, we prepared for Shabbat and we lit candles before sunset. As we looked at our meager meal of "traveling food," we heard the sounds of people overhead singing the welcoming melodies for Shabbat. At first we couldn't believe our ears, but my husband went upstairs to explore. Sure enough, he saw Shabbat candles glowing through the window.

Together we went upstairs and knocked on the door. We were invited inside for a wonderful Shabbat meal with a Jewish Panamanian family. Amazing!! —P.Z.M.

5. It is customary to give *tzedakah*, a gift of charity, each week prior to Shabbat. Some people put coins in a tzedakah box each week and when it is full give it to the synagogue or a specific social service agency. Other opportunities for weekly tzedakah include: giving food to a local food pantry, volunteering at a school, soup kitchen, hospital, or visiting the sick or elderly. Think of other activities and integerate tzedakah into your life.

6. The break from the workweek offers individuals the opportunity to catch up on their quiet time away from the rush of modern life. It is common to hear people say, "Only two more days until Shabbat" or, "I'm so glad tomorrow is Shabbat."

Some people find Shabbat a good time to augment their spiritual, intellectual, and physical life. Meditation, reading, study, and exercise can all be activities that are separate from the workaday world. You may find these enriching as you celebrate Shabbat.

7. Extended family—that is, extend your self to distant cousins and friends and welcome them into your circle for Shabbat. If they see it is fun and meaningful for you, they might try it themselves and even invite you to their home!

8. Feel free to make your own customs for Shabbat that are unique to your household. Is there a special type of art that you are interested in? Explore it each Shabbat. Is hiking your thing? Include it in your family Shabbat experiences. Bring along challah and wine, recite the blessings under the trees. Bring Shabbat into your life, and Shabbat will enhance you.

IF YOU LIVE IN THE HINTERLANDS . . .

Although the vast majority of Jews in America live in major metropolitan areas with access to synagogues and other Jewish institutions, many Jews also live in small towns and other places isolated from the mainstream of American Jewish life. How can those of you in such places create a sense of Shabbat with few Jews and few resources?

Jewish people are a creative sort. So, often in far-flung places, Jews have created small synagogues, meeting in someone's home or a public building. A rabbi is not needed for services, and often people rotate leadership roles.

We know of a small mountain community in which one couple placed an advertisement in the local newspaper to locate Jewish neighbors. They began with a Hanukkah party, which drew people in beyond expectation, followed by home Shabbat dinners. At a Havdalah ceremony, one member baked a special cake decorated with the inscription: "I don't feel so lonely anymore."

Do not hestitate to create what you need. You do not have to have formal Jewish training. Gather books, catalogues, videos, and musical tapes as resources. See references throughout this book and go for it!

RECIPES

Preparations

Because work is traditionally not done on Shabbat, Fridays are often a hectic time in Jewish households as enough food is prepared to last throughout Shabbat. Many people flock to bakeries on Friday mornings to buy their challah and Shabbat desserts. But if you like to avoid lines, you can always buy these items ahead of time, enough even for several weeks, and freeze them.

Nowadays, with the proliferation of two-career families, there is more and more "convenience" food. In major Jewish areas you can often buy prepared Shabbat food from a caterer, or buy frozen items in your local grocery store.

But if you are one of those people who like to cook, here are several basic Shabbat recipes. Plan ahead and enjoy!

MICKEY'S CHALLAH

2 pkg. Quick Rising Yeast
1 cup lukewarm water
2 Tbsp. honey
¼ cup margarine (stick softened to room temperature)

4 large eggs, beaten (set aside 3 Tbsp. of beaten egg for brushing loaves)
1 tsp. salt
6–7 cups unbleached white flour

Combine water and yeast. Let the yeast dissolve for 5 minutes. Add honey and eggs. Let stand 10–15 minutes until mixture forms bubbles on surface. Beat in salt and margarine and 2 cups of flour. Gradually add remaining flour into mix.

If kneading by hand, knead 10–15 minutes until the dough is uniformly smooth and sticky. If using a dough hook, keep mixing until dough wraps around hook. Place the dough in an oiled bowl and cover with a towel.

Store in a warm place until doubled in bulk. Punch down and let rise again. When doubled in bulk a second time, punch down and turn out to knead.

Divide dough into three sections and knead. Roll into snakes and then braid the three snakes together. Once challah is braided, set aside until doubled. Brush with the remaining egg. Bake at 375 degrees for 30–45 minutes.

CHICKEN SOUP

whole chicken, cut into 8ths	*1 parsnip*
3 onions	*1 tsp. fresh dill*
5–6 carrots	*3 quarts water*
5–6 celery stalks	*salt, pepper, and garlic to taste*

Put all ingredients in the pot and bring to a boil. Lower heat and simmer for 30 minutes, then skim fat from the soup. Simmer again for an hour. You can strain the chicken and vegetables out of the soup to be used for another dish, or leave it in the soup. You can add noodles, matzah balls, rice, or potatoes to the soup, and enjoy!

VEGGIE CHOLENT

Traditionally made with meat, this cholent is a healthy stew of mixed vegetables and starches that is slowly cooked overnight, making a warm, comforting Shabbat lunch.

1¼ cups kidney beans	*1 tsp. dill weed*
1 cup lentils	*salt, pepper to taste*
water	*3 sliced carrots*
2 medium sliced onions	*3 sliced celery stalks*
2–3 cloves garlic	*5 large quartered potatoes*
½ cup sliced mushrooms	*1 cup dry red wine*
¼ cup olive oil	*2 Tbsp. soy sauce*
½ cup barley	*vegetable stock*

If beans have not presoaked, wash them and cover with water. Bring to a boil. Remove from heat and soak for 90 minutes.

Sauté onions, garlic, and mushrooms with oil in large pot. Add beans, barley, herbs, and spices. Add carrots, celery, potatoes, soy, and wine. Add vegetable stock to cover about 1 inch above the dry foods.

Before Shabbat, cover the pot tightly and place in the oven at 250 degrees. Let it simmer all night until lunch. Easy and good.

SHABBAT BLESSINGS

If Shabbat and a holiday coincide on a Friday night, turn to the specific holiday blessings and follow those instructions.

Introductory meditation to be recited together before candle lighting:

Today we gather to thank God for all the goodness in our lives, for the beauty of nature, for the love we feel for one another, for the Shabbat tradition which we share. May our celebration increase our awareness of your ongoing gifts, O God.

Candle lighting:
    (On Shabbat, light the candles first, then recite the blessing.)

Baruch Ata Adonai Elohaynu Melech Haolam, asher keedshanu b'mitzvotav v'tzivanu l'hadleek ner shel Shabbat.
Blessed are You Adonai, Eternal One, Who enables us to welcome Shabbat by kindling these lights.

Parents' blessing for their children:
    (Place hands on children and recite.)

FOR BOYS:
May God touch you as you strive to live in the image of Ephraim and Menasshe, leaders who carried on our traditions with pride.

FOR GIRLS:
May God touch you as you strive to live in the image of Sarah and Rebeccah, Rachel and Leah, leaders who carried on our traditions with pride.

CONTINUE SAYING FOR BOTH:

May the Eternal bless you and keep you.
May the Eternal bring you warmth and protect you.
May the Eternal embrace you and grant you peace. Amen.

Evening Kiddush:

> (Raise wine cups and recite. Then drink the wine.)

We praise God with this symbol of fullness, and give thanks for the opportunities we have to share life's blessings.

Baruch Ata Adonai Elohaynu Melech Haolam, boray p'ree hagafen.
Blessed are You Adonai, Eternal One, Who creates fruit from the vine.

Baruch Ata Adonai Elohaynu Melech Haolam, asher keedshanu b'meetzvotav v'rah-zah banu, v'Shabbat kodsho b'ahavah oov'rahzon heen'heelanu, zeekahron l'maasay b'raysheet. Kee hoo yom t'heela l'meekrah-ay kodesh, zaycher l'tzeeat meetzraheem. Kee vanu vacharta ohtanu keedashta meekol ha-ahmeem v'Shabbat kodshecha b'aha-vah oov'ratzon heenaltanu. Baruch Ata Adonai M'kadesh HaShabbat.

Blessed are You Adonai, Eternal One, Who sanctifies us with holy acts, and gives us special times and seasons for rejoicing. Shabbats remind us of the times for celebration, recalling the days of creation of the world and rest from that work. Shabbat is also a liberating time, reminding us of the exodus from Egyptian slavery. You have distinguished us from all people, and have given us the Shabbat full of joy and inspiration. Blessed are You Adonai, Eternal One, Who sanctifies the Shabbat.

Saturday Lunch Kiddush:

> (Raise wine cups and recite. Then drink the wine.)

Al ken bayrah Adonai et Yom Hashabbat v'kodsho.
Baruch Ata Adonai Elohaynu Melech Haolam, boray p'ree hagafen.
Behold, the Eternal blessed the seventh day and called it a holy time.
Blessed are You Adonai, Eternal One, Who creates fruit from the vine.

Blessing over the challah:

> (Remove challah cover and recite. Then give each person a piece of bread.)

Baruch Ata Adonai Elohaynu Melech Haolam, hamotzi lechem meen ha-aretz.
Blessed are You Adonai, Eternal One, Who creates bread from the earth.

2
ROSH HASHANAH— THE NEW YEAR

In the seventh month, on the first day of the month, you shall observe a holy day; you shall not work at your occupations. You shall observe it as a day when the shofar is trumpeted (Numbers 29:1).

THE holiday of Rosh Hashanah, the Jewish New Year, begins the autumn season filled with Jewish holidays. This holy day of blowing the *shofar,* the ram's horn, is based on several biblical references and heralds the new year.

Rosh Hashanah, which literally means the head of the year, arrives in September or October, depending on the particular year. It is celebrated as a two-day holiday in most communities, including Israel, although some Reform and Reconstructionist synagogues celebrate only one day.

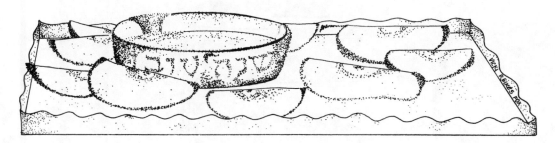

Rosh Hashanah is a new year's celebration unlike a secular American new year. It is serious, yet also joyous. The Jewish new year is one that emphasizes a personal spiritual renewal linked with an ancient form of prayer and personal reflection. It is a time when Jews pray for a year of life and health for themselves, their loved ones, and the whole world.

The Jewish new year requires Jews to stop the pace of busy lives by shutting out other distractions and focusing on renewing ties with family and friends. The new year emphasizes the creation of the world and challenges people to consider this and other beginning moments.

We take stock of our lives. We ask: Where are we now in our relationships and our goals? Where are we going? This process of introspection known as the Ten Days of Awe begins at Rosh Hashanah and continues through Yom Kippur, the Day of Atonement.

GREETINGS

Most Jewish holidays have unique greetings. *"L'shana Tovah Tikatayvu*—May you be inscribed for life in the New Year"* is the greeting for Rosh Hashanah. Or one can simply say *"L'shana Tovah*—Happy New Year."*

This greeting focuses on the essence of the holiday: Each individual wishes for life in the new year. The phrase acknowledges the unspoken Divine role in this plan. Jews ask that God, the Judge and Source of all life, grant life, health, and fulfillment in this coming year.

HOME TRADITIONS

Preparing for the Holiday

In preparation for Rosh Hashanah, consider everything that can be accomplished in the days before the holiday. Buy round *challahs,* apples and honey, wine for *Kiddush,* and candles. Plan for the giving of *tzedakah,* a gift of money or time for a charitable cause, as you plan holiday meal menus and invite guests.

The table for Rosh Hashanah holiday meals is set with an especially nice tablecloth, candlesticks, wine, round challah, and apples and honey. Use fresh flowers to decorate the table.

While Judaism encourages the giving of tzedakah throughout all seasons, on Rosh Hashanah this act of generosity takes on greater significance. In the Rosh Hashanah liturgy, tzedakah is one of the three ways in which a person can influence God, as the Eternal judges the merits of each person and determines if that person is "written into the Book of Life."

There are many opportunities for giving tzedakah before the holiday. It can be given to social agencies or individuals, food pantries, schools, and hospitals. You can give a gift to any cause whose values you believe in, whether it is a specifically Jewish cause or not.

Evening

As with Shabbat, Rosh Hashanah begins at night with the lighting of two candles and the recitation of the blessing. This occurs with the setting of the sun or when sitting down to dinner. Some families follow candle lighting with a blessing for their children.

Next the *Shehehayanu* prayer is recited, acknowledging the privilege of having reached this time of the new year together.

At the dinner table the wine is blessed first. Kiddush, the prayer over the wine, is recited over a full cup. For Rosh Hashanah the wording and even the music of this prayer is slightly different from the Shabbat version. This special Kiddush emphasizes that Rosh Hashanah is the day of creation, the day of remembrance, and the day of the shofar sounding.

The challah, a twisted egg or white bread, is baked specially for Rosh Hashanah in round loaves rather than the usual oblong shape used for weekly Shabbat meals. The round loaves represent the continuous seasons of the year and the cycles of time.

The prayer over the challah is recited, and then pieces of the challah are distributed to be dipped by each person into honey before eating. The table ritual is concluded as apple slices are individually dipped in honey, which represents sweetness and hope for the new year.

At the beginning of the meal, some Sephardic Jews eat fish, leaving the head of the fish on the plate, to symbolize a wish for prosperity and good luck in the coming year. They also add special blessings for other fruits and vegetables, all symbolic of different wishes for the new year.

At the conclusion of the meal the *Birkat Hamazon,* the thanksgiving prayer, is sung.

Second Evening

The same rituals are repeated the second night of Rosh Hashanah, including the Shehehayanu prayer. In some homes, after eating apples and honey, people also eat special, unique fruits not eaten yet during the year, such as figs, kumquats, pomegranates, and papaya. These are called Shehehayanu fruits, fruits that highlight the uniqueness of Rosh Hashanah on the second day of the holiday.

Daytime

Based on an understanding of the biblical verse that defines aspects of Rosh Hashanah, it is a tradition to celebrate the holiday at home and in the synagogue with family and friends. It is a time to refrain from work. "In the seventh month on the first day of the month, you shall observe a complete rest" (Leviticus 23:23). All who are able should not work or attend school on this day.

After morning synagogue services on both days, people gather for a festive lunch. At the table they recite a shorter version of the blessing over the wine and then the blessings over challah and the apples and honey. The Birkat Hamazon follows the conclusion of the meal, and then the afternoon is enjoyed by socializing and relaxing.

SYNAGOGUE TRADITIONS

Rosh Hashanah is a community holiday, and much of its celebration occurs within a synagogue. Although the various movements within Judaism (Conservative, Orthodox, Reconstructionist, and Reform) reflect different beliefs about theology and practice of Jewish life, each welcomes the new year with introspection and with common themes of renewal and hope.

Slichot, a preparatory forgiveness service, is held at midnight the Saturday night before Rosh Hashanah. At this service, the holiday pleas for forgiveness, recited throughout the Days of Awe, are heard for the first time.

On Rosh Hashanah the prayerbook used is known as the *Machzor.* The intent of this word indicates the hope that people turn and change within the High Holiday period—the Days of Awe. Some synagogues provide a Machzor for each congregant; other synagogues require you to bring your own. Be sure to check ahead of time if you are attending a synagogue's holiday services for the first time so you won't find yourself without a prayerbook.

For the entire Ten Days of Awe, the synagogue itself looks different. The *Torah* coverings are changed from their everyday colors to white. The same transformation to white is seen on the cover on the reader's stand and the Ark curtain. In addition, cantors and rabbis are dressed in *kittels,* white robes. White is a symbol of purity, and as we approach God during these days of introspection we do so with a pure heart.

Temple Membership

In almost all synagogues throughout the country, Rosh Hashanah and Yom Kippur are the two holidays for which it is necessary to call the temple in advance of the holidays and join the synagogue as a member to participate in the holiday services. At times, holiday tickets are available for nonmembers who are visiting or have just moved into town.

While it is true that any person is welcome to attend services throughout the rest of the year without being a member of a congregation, synagogue membership is important year round. It is crucial that the synagogue, supported by its members, be there to meet individual needs: for support at death, for celebration at births, for marriage ceremonies. The temple is also needed to meet community goals: for Jewish education, for enrichment for children or adults, and for a political presence.

If you are unable to locate a synagogue to join, you may call the national headquarters of the Conservative, Orthodox, Reconstructionist, or Reform movements (see Appendix, p. 155) for a temple near you. Often congregations advertise in Jewish newspapers or local papers in the weeks preceding the new year; also check the Yellow Pages for congregations.

Shofar

The shofar is a specially cleaned, treated, and hollowed horn, usually a ram's horn, which carries the potential for deep sounds and high notes. The shofar was sounded in ancient times to declare significant occasions, such as the new moon of each month of the Jewish calendar, the start of the holidays, and special events such as a call for war.

According to tradition, blasting of the shofar occurred as God gave the Torah to the Israelites at Mount Sinai, and the blasting of the shofar occurs whenever Jews are judged by God. The peculiar crying sound of the shofar is a unique symbol for the new year.

The whole congregation stands each time the piercing cry is sounded, and three specific sounds are repeated many times totaling one hundred shofar notes, ending with a final, elongated note.

It has been a tradition to bring the shofar to homebound people who are unable to go to synagogue so that they too may hear the shrill cry. Volunteer shofar blowers go to the homes of shut-ins or to hospitals to fulfill this *mitzvah,* good deed.

The month preceding Rosh Hashanah is set aside to practice blowing the shofar. During this period the shofar is blown at weekday services in synagogues throughout the country, including services at Jewish camps, and in many households this skill is practiced daily. As people practice, the high notes and the breathy sounds remind them of the hard work that entering the new year demands of each Jew.

Services

The evening service welcomes the holiday and sets the mood. It is a custom in the Orthodox community to attend services early in the evening prior to the holiday meal. Conservative, Reform, and Reconstructionist synagogues begin the evening service after the festive meal.

The morning service contains the major themes of Rosh Hashanah. The Torah reading for the first day describes the matriarch Sarah's fulfillment of her wish for a child. The reading for the second day describes the patriarch Abraham's trial as he responds to God's call. The service is punctuated with the blowing of the shofar.

Central Prayers for the Holiday

Three central prayers in the Rosh Hashanah service focus on the holiday's special themes: *Avinu Malkaynu, Unetaneh Tokef,* and the *Musaf Amidah.*

Repetition of Avinu Malkaynu, Our Parent, Our Sovereign, occurs throughout Rosh Hashanah and Yom Kippur. It is an emotional, highly melodic, eerie-sounding prayer in which Jewish people turn to God. They ask for forgiveness, for protection, for blessings.

This prayer dates from between the second and sixth centuries and includes forty-four requests for God's help in life. The prayer reflects on God as the Source of all Life, the Eternal One, and also acknowledges the Power that is Divine, the Ruler that determines life and death.

Unetaneh Tokef describes the moment in which God judges each individual. The prayer is emotional and dramatic; it is expressed through poetry and eerie music: "On Rosh Hashanah our destiny is written; at the end of Yom Kippur it is sealed. Who shall live and who shall die? Who by fire and who by water?" God determines beginnings and endings and yet human beings struggle to influence the Divine decree.

The prayer continues: "But personal renewal, prayer, and charity avert the harsh

decree." This reflects the hope that individual actions will influence the Divine to grant life for the next year.

The *Musaf Amidah,* known in Reform synagogues as Service for the Sounding of the Shofar, includes the blowing of the shofar. It accents the three themes found in its three sections. *Malchuiot* (Rulership) proclaims God's eternal power over all the earth; *Zichronot* (Memory) stresses the historical experiences of the Jewish people which God remembers as God judges each individual; and *Shofarot* (Blessing of the Ram's Horn) emphasizes the giving of the Torah at Mount Sinai with the accompanying sounding of the shofar.

THE ROSH HASHANAH FASHION PARADE

When I was a little girl growing up in the small town of Elgin, Illinois, the holidays of Rosh Hashanah and Yom Kippur were a wonderful time for me to see all the women decked out in their holiday best. Life in a small town did not afford frequent opportunities to observe such clothes, hats, and jewelry. To me this was part of the excitement of the holidays.

Only when I was older did I learn that there was a reason for all this "dressing up." Rosh Hashanah was the start of a new year, a new chance to set our lives on the right track. And it was only proper to appear ready for those changes. This wasn't merely a fashion parade: New and special attire had an important purpose after all!

—P.Z.M.

INSIGHTS

Rosh Hashanah Names

Rosh Hashanah, besides meaning the head of the year, is also known by other names that highlight specific concepts that are key to the holiday:

Yom Harat Olam—The Birth Day of the World

According to Jewish tradition, the creation of the world occurred on Rosh Hashanah, which is also the first day of the Jewish month of *Tishre*. Jews acknowledge the birth of the universe as they welcome each new year.

"When was the earth created?" asked the rabbis. "When human beings could acknowledge it." The actual dating of the beginning of creation is *not* what is commemorated. Rather, Jews commemorate and celebrate that there was a beginning. That beginning gives opportunities for new beginnings as human beings.

Each Jewish new year begins another year in the Jewish calendar. The numbering is a Jewish measure of years since the moment of creation forward. The Rosh Hashanah that begins in the fall of 1992 coincides with the Jewish year 5753. Included in the appendix is a listing of the Jewish calendar dates through 2005.

Yom Hadin—The Judgment Day

Rosh Hashanah is the day when God begins the process of examining the life of each Jew over the past year. An ancient legend envisions God judging the world and each individual on this day (*Talmud Babli,* Rosh Hashanah, 16b). Each person is responsible for his/her actions and is weighed according to his/her behaviors.

Rosh Hashanah is not only the day when God judges. It is also the day in which individuals search their souls and evaluate their own lives.

There are three concrete ways to change: through *tshuvah*—personal religious renewal; *tfillah*—prayer and introspection; and *tzedakah*—good deeds and gifts of charity.

Yom Zikaron—Day of Remembrance

Rosh Hashanah is the holiday in which God remembers each individual and when Jews remember their essence as a people. It is a holiday that encourages us to remember families, traditions, and identity.

Yom HaTruah—Day of the Shofar Blast

As a human monarch celebrates his/her coronation with drama and sound, so the Divine celebrates the Monarchy each year at Rosh Hashanah. The sound of the shofar allows the spirit of the holidays to enter each individual not through word or activity but through an experience of pure, natural sound.

Repentance Is Possible

The High Holiday cycle emphasizes that repentance is possible for all people. It reassures Jews that they can achieve forgiveness even if they are stubborn, reluctant, defiant, maybe even unbelieving. Judaism emphasizes that all human beings have an opportunity to explore and transform their lives. That optimism is the essence of the Days of Awe.

Bonds Between Parents and Children

The *Akedah,* a Torah portion read on Rosh Hashanah, describes the biblical scene in which Abraham responds to God's call to sacrifice his son. Isaac is spared after God sees that Abraham was willing to obey the command; a ram is sacrificed in Isaac's stead.

Today we consider how to live life to the fullest without sacrificing children's needs for parental love and stability. In the ever increasingly complex world, this theme is a challenge for each parent to consider in the new year.

ACTIVITIES

1. Preparing for spiritual renewal:

a. Ask yourself: What have I learned in the last year? What am I looking forward to in this year? What are my personal goals?

b. Make a large family chart and discuss similarities and differences of what you have learned and what are your goals. Do parents comment on different things they have learned than children do? What do those differences tell you? What can family members learn from each other?

2. In the last century the tradition of sending Rosh Hashanah greeting cards has blossomed. Of course the influence of the greeting card business has touched the Jewish community, but aside from that it is a way for family and friends to send each other wishes for the coming year.

a. Purchasing cards is one way to send greetings.

b. Design your own logo or special decoration and make your own greeting card. Use construction paper to cut out symbols of the holiday and paste onto background material of card stock. Look at the illustrations in this chapter for examples. You can add a "growing family" picture to personalize the greeting even more.

c. You can also write a Rosh Hashanah update every year to send to family and friends. This is a good occasion to write of changes in your lives, issues of concern, and joyous moments.

3. The Rosh Hashanah dinner table can be a wonderful place for sharing on the holiday.

a. Besides special friends and family, you can invite visiting college students, new community members, single adults, single parents and their children, and recent immigrants.

b. Storytelling can be a great addition to the Rosh Hashanah dinner or lunch. Stories can highlight Rosh Hashanahs in other countries or previous years' memories. They might even have a moral or pose a difficult question.

c. Over Rosh Hashanah lunch after morning services one person might begin to discuss an aspect of the Torah portion or a point of the sermon delivered at the synagogue. This can lead to a lively discussion right through to dessert.

d. Discussions during holiday meals may reflect different generations' experiences. What was it like growing up and marking Rosh Hashanah in New York? in Teheran? in Vienna? in Moscow? in Elgin, Illinois? in Fullerton, California? Share those differing backgrounds and experiences; the richness and variety of experiences in growing up Jewish will surprise you.

4. Another focus is the opportunity to give each person a blessing. Again, going around the table, one person can begin by asking the person sitting next to her, "What would you like to be blessed with in this year?" After the response, the blesser continues, "May you be blessed with . . . _____ in this upcoming year." This experience can be moving. It also takes the concept of blessing and expands it from only parents blessing children, or rabbis blessing congregants, to a broader experience of blessings that we can give to one another.

5. Books to consider reading for the holiday for young children may include: *Gates of Awe, High Holiday Prayers for Young Children* by R. Orkand, J. Orkand, H. Bogot, (New York: Central Conference of American Rabbis, 1991); *Hear, O Israel: About Learning* by Molly Cone (New York: Union of American Hebrew Congregations, 1971); *Stories for Children* by Isaac Bashevis Singer (New York: Farrar/Strauss/Giroux, 1985). Books for adults may include: *Modern Hebrew Poetry*, edited and translated by Ruth Finer Mintz (Los Angeles: University of California Press, 1966); *Where Heaven and Earth Touch* by Danny Siegel (Northvale, New Jersey: Jason Aronson, Inc., 1989).

RECIPES

Preparing the Rosh Hashanah meals can be one way to participate and contribute to the holiday. Special holiday meals may include foods from the Ashkenazic traditions coming from such countries as Germany, Poland, and Russia, and foods from the Sephardic traditions coming from such countries as Turkey, Greece, and Morocco. Each culture in which Jewish people live influences aspects of Jewish traditions, and this is true particularly with food.

SARA'S SWEET-AND-SOUR SALMON

3 or 4 salmon steaks	*small handful of sugar*
2 white sliced onions	*bay leaf*
¾ cup mild vinegar	*peppercorns*
2 cups water	*two handfuls raisins*

Buy 3 or 4 thinly cut salmon steaks. Cut them in half. Cover them with two sliced white onions. Next make the brine: mix vinegar, water, sugar, bay leaf, peppercorns, and raisins. Simmer the brine until it boils. Pour it over the fish. Cover the fish and put it in the oven for 30 minutes at 350 degrees. Make it several days in advance so it can soak in the spices.

Sephardic Stuffed Zucchini

4 fresh zucchini
1 lb. ground beef, veal, or turkey
½ cup chopped parsley
1 finely chopped onion
2 Tbsp. matzah meal
2 Tbsp. sugar

juice of 2 lemons
1 can tomato puree
1½ cups water
2 tsp. cumin
salt and pepper to taste

Cut each zucchini into 2 three-inch pieces. Scoop out each piece (saving the insides), leaving the shell for stuffing. Mix meat, parsley, onion, cumin, matzah meal, salt and pepper to taste. Stuff the meat mixture into the zucchini shells. Put all the zucchini scooping into the bottom of a large pot. Arrange the stuffed zucchini in the pot. Pour the tomato puree over it. Add the sugar and lemon juice with the water. Cover and bring to a boil on a high flame, then reduce to a medium flame. Cook for ½ hour and serve with spiced rice.

Himmel and Erde—The Heavens and the Earth

(A German Rosh Hashanah food symbolizing the relationship between people on the earth and God above.)

2 lbs. white potatoes
2 lbs. green apples

½ cup margarine
1 cup honey

Cut apples and potatoes into slices. Layer the slices of potatoes and apples alternately in a glass dish. Dot with margarine and honey. Cover with foil paper. Bake at 400 degrees for an hour. Should be soft and juicy.

ROSH HASHANAH BLESSINGS

Introductory meditation to be recited together before candle lighting:

Today we gather to thank God for all the goodness in our lives, for the beauty of nature, for the love we feel for one another, for the Rosh Hashanah tradition which we share.
May our celebration increase our awareness of your ongoing gifts, O God.

Candle lighting:
(Recite this blessing, then light the candles. If it is also Shabbat, light the candles first, then recite the blessing.)

Baruch Ata Adonai Elohaynu Melech Haolam, asher keedshanu b'mitzvotav v'tzivanu l'hadleek ner shel (Shabbat v') Yom Tov.
Blessed are You Adonai, Eternal One, Who enables us to welcome (Shabbat and) Rosh Hashanah by kindling these lights.

Shehehayanu:
(On the first night of Rosh Hashanah add:)
Baruch Ata Adonai Elohaynu Melech Haolam, shehehayanu, v'keeyomanu v'higeeyanu laz'man hazeh.
Blessed are You Adonai, Eternal One, Who has kept us alive, sustained us, and encouraged us to celebrate this New Year.

Parents' blessing for their children:
(Place hands on children and recite.)

FOR BOYS:
May God touch you as you strive to live in the image of Ephraim and Menasshe, leaders who carried on our traditions with pride.

FOR GIRLS:
May God touch you as you strive to live in the image of Sarah and Rebeccah, Rachel and Leah, leaders who carried on our traditions with pride.

CONTINUE SAYING FOR BOTH:
May the Eternal bless you and keep you.
May the Eternal bring you warmth and protect you.
May the Eternal embrace you and grant you peace. Amen.

Rosh Hashanah Evening Kiddush to be used for holiday nights and Shabbat:
    (Raise wine cups and recite. Then drink the wine.)

We praise God with this symbol of fullness, and give thanks for the opportunities we have to share life's blessings.

Baruch Ata Adonai Elohaynu Melech Haolam, boray p'ree hagafen.
Blessed are You Adonai, Eternal One, Who creates fruit from the vine.

Baruch Ata Adonai Elohaynu Melech Haolam, asher bachar banu meekol ahm, v'romemanu meekol lashon, v'keedshanu b'meetzvotav. V'teetayn lanu, Adonai Elohaynu, b'ahavah (Shabbatot leemnucha oo) moadeem l'seemcha, chageem u'z-maneem l'sasson et yom (haShabbat hazeh v'et) yom hazeekaron hazeh, yom truah, mikrah kodesh zaycher l'tzeeat meetzrayim. Kee banu bacharta v'otanu keedashta meekol ha-ahmeem, (v'Shabbat oo) moaday kodshecha (b'ahavah oo'vratzon) b'seemcha oo'vsasson heenhaltanu. Baruch Ata Adonai M'kadesh (haShabbat v') Yisrael, v'hazmaneem.

Blessed are You Adonai, Eternal One, Who has chosen us from among all people, sanctified us with holy acts, and given special times and seasons for rejoicing. (Shabbat and) Rosh Hashanah remind us of the times for celebration, recalling this day filled with the call of the shofar and its many memories. You have distinguished us from all people, and have given us (the Shabbat and) holy festivals, full of joy and inspiration. Blessed are You Adonai, Eternal One, Who sanctifies (the Shabbat,) the people Israel, and our sacred seasons.

Daytime Kiddush:
(Raise wine cups and recite. Then drink the wine.)

El Moaday Adonai Meekrah-ay kodesh, asher teekrehoo otam b'moadam. VayDaber Moshe et moaday Adonai el b'nay Yisrael.

These are the sacred times appointed by God; and you shall announce them in their season.

Baruch Ata Adonai Elohaynu Melech Haolam, boray p'ree hagafen.

Blessed are You Adonai, Eternal One, Who creates fruit from the vine.

Blessing over the challah:

Baruch Ata Adonai Elohaynu Melech Haolam, hamotzi lechem meen ha-aretz.

Blessed are You Adonai, Eternal One, Who creates bread from the earth.

Blessing over the apples and honey:
(Dip apple slices in honey and recite. Then eat the slices.)

Baruch Ata Adonai Elohaynu Melech Haolam, boray p'ree ha aytz.

Blessed are You Adonai, Eternal One, Who creates fruit from the trees.

Eternal, our God, and God of all people, make this new year sweet and good for all.

3
YOM KIPPUR—
WE ASK FORGIVENESS

Y OM Kippur, the Day of Atonement, occurs in early fall ten days after Rosh Hashanah. The last of the Days of Awe, it is a day to "atone for one's sins" and ask forgiveness for one's past failings.

This major holy day does not recall a specific Jewish historical event. Rather, it is experienced personally as a spiritual challenge involving reevaluation and change. Yom Kippur is one of the most difficult and soul-searching days of the year. It requires the ability to stand before God—and oneself; it demands the honesty to admit mistakes and to appeal for forgiveness.

Yom Kippur is a day of complete concentration. This is accomplished through fasting; no food or drink is consumed for twenty-five hours. The fast is based on the biblical phrase "For on this day, you shall practice self-denial/self-control." This total abstinence blocks out distractions and allows a directed focus on the task of repentance.

All healthy adults are required to fast. There are special laws pertaining to sick individuals, pregnant women, and women who have just given birth. Although children may practice fasting while they are younger, they are expected to begin fasting by age thirteen.

GREETINGS

The different greetings for Yom Kippur embody the various themes of the holiday: People say in Hebrew, *"G'mar Hatimah Tovah,"* which means, "May you be sealed for life the upcoming year." (A short form is *"G'mar Tov."*)

People will also greet each other by saying in Hebrew, *"Tzom Kal,"* which means, "May you have an easy fast." In addition, it is always appropriate to wish someone in Yiddish a *"Gut Yontif"* or in Hebrew *"Hag Sameach,"* both of which mean "Good Holiday."

HOME TRADITIONS

The meal eaten before the start of Yom Kippur is festive, and takes place quite early to allow people to get to synagogue before sunset. The *Kiddush,* the prayer over the wine, is not recited, although the blessing over the uncovered bread is recited and round *challah* is eaten with honey. (The bread is uncovered for this holiday only because the blessing is not preceded by Kiddush.)

Because this is the last meal eaten for twenty-five hours, it is important to plan a meal that will sustain you. Many people believe that salty foods will make the fast harder, so salty foods are avoided before the fast. Others believe starchy food will make the fast easier because carbohydrates last longer. If you are a caffeine drinker, consider giving up caffeine for approximately one week before Yom Kippur to make the fast easier. Do whatever works for you and be sure to drink plenty of water before the start of the fast.

Just before leaving for the synagogue, several rituals are completed. It is customary to first light *Yizkor* candles, or memorial candles, for those in the family who are

deceased, although a blessing is not said when lighting these candles. (These special candles, which burn the entire twenty-five hours, can be purchased ahead of time at synagogues or Jewish stores.)

Then two holiday candles are lit and blessed *after* rather than before the meal. Lighting of the candles signals the beginning of Yom Kippur, and no eating or drinking occurs after the onset of the holiday. Parents bless their children for health and life in the new year. Finally, before leaving for the synagogue, Jews recite the *Shehehayanu,* the prayer praising God for having reached the season of introspection.

Additional Yom Kippur customs besides the fast were formulated by the rabbis, the codifiers of Jewish law. The rabbis expanded the concept of self-denial as it related to certain personal behaviors: not wearing any leather goods, not bathing, not using oils, makeup, or perfumes, not engaging in sexual relations on Yom Kippur. These limitations are practiced to enhance the inner spiritual awareness on Yom Kippur.

Another traditional custom is to wear white clothes on this holiday to symbolize a desire for purification and renewal. As you approach the synagogue at the beginning of Yom Kippur, you may notice men and women wearing white suits and dresses.

At the conclusion of the fast, it is traditional to have a "break fast." Some synagogues offer a light meal at the conclusion of Yom Kippur services. Others offer glasses of orange juice to "jump-start" congregants on their way home for "break fasts." (See the recipe on page 53 for a "break fast" *kugel.*)

SYNAGOGUE TRADITIONS

There is always a sense of urgency for those arriving at synagogue to attend *Kol Nidre,* the service that begins Yom Kippur. Friends and family greet each other and hurry in to take their seats in time for the opening notes of this dramatic service.

Kol Nidre

The custom of reciting Kol Nidre, the Absolution of All Vows, at the start of Yom Kippur began somewhere between the second and sixth centuries.

The Yom Kippur service begins with a plea for the remission of vows for the upcoming year. This is curious. Why should Jews appeal to God for the upcoming year rather than approach God to absolve their vows for the past year?

Throughout the centuries Jews lived in political situations in which their very lives were at stake. Sometimes they were forced to deny their Judaism and pledge allegiance to a different faith. The mechanism of Kol Nidre realized the precarious nature of Jewish life and provided a release for whatever religious vows these Jews might be forced to make during the upcoming year to ensure their physical survival.

Kol Nidre is restricted to vows which concern the relationship between the human being and God. It does not cancel personal, political, or business obligations.

The drama of this judgment scene can be felt by each individual. All stand as the *Torahs* are taken out of the ark. The eerie call of the music evokes tears as it is repeated three times, swelling to its poignant conclusion. The words evoke recognition of the unique relationship between God and the Jewish people. The memories of the past move individuals to feelings of longing and love.

The particular melody used by most Ashkenazic congregations first appeared among Jews of Southern Germany between the fifteenth and sixteenth centuries (A. Z. Idelsohn, "The Kol Nidre Tune," *Hebrew Union College Annual,* 1931–32). Sephardic and other Jews of Oriental lands recite Kol Nidre in a less dramatic melody.

Services During the Day of Yom Kippur

Services for Yom Kippur day contain various sections. Parts of the Torah are read twice, once in the morning and once in the late afternoon. Although services continue basically all day long, there is usually a break before the afternoon service. Some people gather for study sessions or discussions; others go home for a rest.

Confessional

The *Vidui,* the confessional and recitation of sins, is repeated many times in the Yom Kippur liturgy, although the particular number of repetitions varies with individual prayerbook editions. This recitation follows a similar structure whether the confessional is recited in a Reform or Conservative, Orthodox or Reconstructionist synagogue. Although the melodies may vary, the music is always powerful, flowing from a deep, blasting call to God to a humble, repetitive communal listing of sins.

The confessional concludes with a gentler melody in which the whole congregation joins in asking: "For all these sins, forgiving God, forgive us, pardon us, grant us atonement" (J. Harlow, *Mahzor for Rosh Hashanah and Yom Kippur: A Prayerbook for the Days of Awe,* New York: Rabbinical Assembly, 1972, p. 381).

The confessional begins by acknowledging that human beings accept their responsibilities and imperfections: "We are not so brazen or so arrogant as to say that we are perfect and have not sinned. For indeed we have sinned." The prayer continues as congregants communally recite an alphabetical listing of human failures. These failures stress corruption in business, in politics, in love.

The whole of the confessional is recited in a plural form in public prayer. All the community stands responsible and vulnerable before God. Jews are not singled out for individual errors; rather they are allowed privacy in the communal confessional.

The prayer concludes by imploring God to forgive all Jews for transgressions. The congregants humbly appeal to God for compassion and understanding.

Memorial Service

Yizkor, the memorial service for the dead, is recited several times a year and is a particularly emotional moment of Yom Kippur. Many people will enter the synagogue just before Yizkor to ensure their presence in memory of and respect for the dead. Orthodox and some Conservative synagogues recite Yizkor after the Torah service in the morning. Reform and other liberal synagogues will read Yizkor near the conclusion of Yom Kippur in the late afternoon.

Some Jews think that only those whose parents, children, spouses, or siblings have died should remain in the sanctuary during Yizkor. However, in many communities today all congregants remain standing together not only to remember their personal deceased but also to remember Jewish martyrs, and Kaddish, the memorial prayer for the dead, is recited for all of them.

The Concluding Service

Neilah, the concluding service, is recited when the sun is setting and the evening shadows begin to emerge. It is the final opportunity on Yom Kippur to ask for forgiveness.

The word Neilah itself means closing. Some interpret this to mean that the gates of the heavens are closing, that the opportunities for confession and forgiveness are ending. Despite that imposed ending, we continue to pray for life in the New Year. Neilah concludes with the long, final blasting of the shofar, which is only blown on Yom Kippur at this final dramatic moment.

As congregants stream out of temple to break the fast, there is a tremendous feeling of relief that the day is ended and the prayers have been accepted. People hug and kiss each other joyfully as they once again wish each other a happy new year.

INSIGHTS

Fasting

The most widely known custom concerning Yom Kippur is the twenty-five-hour total fast. Praying with an empty stomach allows total focus as Jews examine the depths of their souls. Jews move from the physical world to that of the spiritual.

Fasting creates a sense of self-denial and self-control: If I can resist my hunger for food for one day, can I have strength to resist my hunger for things, for power, for control?

Fasting also teaches what it means to be hungry. You can experience in a microcosm what life might be like without the sources that support life. And when you conclude this day, you may ask: What can I do to feed the hungry in the world—those who are hungry for food and those who are hungry for emotional, spiritual nurturance?

CHILDREN AND FASTING

When I was little I used to think of Yom Kippur day as an opportunity to feast while my parents were fasting. After all, as they provided only minimal meals for us, my siblings and I would invariably scrounge up various delicious "treats" for ourselves. Now that I have children I have had to rethink what fasting on Yom Kippur should mean for them.

As they approach the age of fasting, children can start "practicing" a little bit of the day, but they should not be encouraged to do a complete fast while they are still under age thirteen. With prior discussion, even young children can be discouraged from looking on Yom Kippur as a day of feasting. Show them that they can eat nourishing but not festive food as their part on this most solemn of Jewish holidays.

—P.Z.M.

Reading the Book of Jonah

On Yom Kippur afternoon it is customary to read the Book of Jonah in the synagogue. This ancient story offers opportunities for contemplation and discussion.

Jonah was drafted into being a prophet. He did not take to the job willingly. God told Jonah to go to the city of Nineveh and make the inhabitants change their evil ways. Reluctantly, Jonah began his journey and only completed his mission after several strange things happened to him.

Adults and children might consider such questions as: How did the violence of the ocean storm during Jonah's voyage frighten the sailors and make them perform an evil act? How could the sailors throw Jonah overboard without caring about his life? Why is the whale such an important dimension of this story? What lengths did Jonah have to go through to make a strange city change its ways? What is so unusual about a whole city changing its ways? We can examine the story and apply the lessons to our own personal life. What one or two changes should we make in our lives? Why is change so hard for most people?

Asking Forgiveness

The *Mishneh*, the first basic codification of Jewish law, reads: "Yom Kippur atones for the sins between human beings and God; however, when people have hurt one another, atonement is not possible until they have made peace with each other" (Mishneh, Yoma 8:9).

Judaism teaches that human beings can make amends with each other—can wipe the slate clean—and each year stand anew before God after having asked forgiveness of others. Wiping the slate clean demands that first an individual is internally aware of his or her mistakes and wrongdoings. It then requires a conscious sorting of words and deeds. And finally an action—a correction or apology—is offered.

One way of begining this process may be to keep a journal that will trace your forgiveness process from Rosh Hashanah to Yom Kippur. Write down your thoughts and feelings, acknowledge your weaknesses, and evaluate your goals for the coming year.

Another step in the process of forgiveness is to approach individuals—family members or close friends—and ask them directly for forgiveness. All of us have encountered unpleasant situations within our work and personal lives. Sometimes things go on between friends that are painful and even embarrassing.

Parents and children might undertake this process together. What are the areas in which parents were weak as individuals? Parents can note times in which they might have acted abruptly or impatiently. Perhaps they even misjudged a child during stressful moments.

The parent can model asking for forgiveness. Parents can say: "Children, I would like to ask your forgiveness for my shortcomings. Can you please forgive me?" Each parent can spend separate time with each child so that the forgiveness process can open intimate communication.

This process of asking for forgiveness is difficult. In many ways, some people find it easier to sit in the synagogue fasting a full day than to approach a lover, a child, a parent, and ask for that person's forgiveness. Imagine the difference in our relationships when we overcome hesitation and experience honesty and resolution as we approach Yom Kippur. By focusing on asking for forgiveness as a process prior to Yom Kippur, the individual can truly be ready to experience the Day of Atonement.

RECIPES

Typically the "break-the-fast" meal is a light dairy meal. It may feature lox and bagels, herring, other fish, and sweets. Orange juice and coffee are always appreciated. *Kugel,* which takes many forms, can be made sweet for this occasion. Here's one such recipe.

STEVE'S BREAK-THE-FAST KUGEL

*1 8 oz. package broad noodles (cooked,
   drained, and cooled)*
1 pint large curd cottage cheese
¾ tsp. vanilla
1½ cups milk
1 cup buttermilk
4–5 eggs (beat just before adding)

½ stick butter, melted
¼ cup sugar

TOPPING:
½ cup cornflakes, crumbled
½ tsp. cinnamon
1 tsp. sugar

Make the day before Yom Kippur begins. Combine kugel ingredients in a large bowl. Add noodles. Mix. Pour into baking dish (glass 9″ × 13″ inch).

Cover and refrigerate overnight. Should be set when chilled. Mix the topping and spread over the kugel. Bake at 350 degrees for 1 hour or until golden brown.

Reheat when coming home from temple after the concluding service.

YOM KIPPUR BLESSINGS

Introductory meditation to be recited together after dinner before candle lighting:

Today we gather to thank God for all the goodness in our lives, for the beauty of nature, for the love we feel for one another, for the Yom Kippur tradition which we share.

May our celebration increase our awareness of your ongoing gifts, O God.

Candle lighting:

  (We recite this blessing, then light the candles.)

Baruch Ata Adonai Elohaynu Melech Haolam, asher keedshanu b'mitzvotav v'tzivanu l'hadleek ner shel (Shabbat v') Yom Hakeepureem.
Blessed are You Adonai, Eternal One, Who enables us to welcome (Shabbat and) Yom Kippur by kindling these lights.

Shehehayanu:
Baruch Ata Adonai Elohaynu Melech Haolam, shehehayanu, v'keeyomanu v'higeeyanu laz'man hazeh.
Blessed are You Adonai, Eternal One, Who has kept us alive, sustained us, and encouraged us to observe this Day of Atonement.

Parents' blessing for their children:

FOR BOYS:
May God touch you as you strive to live in the tradition of Ephraim and Menasshe, leaders who carried our traditions with pride.

FOR GIRLS:

May God touch you as you strive to live in the tradition of Sarah and Rebeccah, Rachel and Leah, leaders who carried our traditions with pride.

CONTINUE BY SAYING:

May the Eternal bless you and keep you.
May the Eternal bring you warmth and protect you.
May the Eternal embrace you and grant you peace. Amen.

4
SUKKOT—THE JEWISH THANKSGIVING FESTIVAL

ONLY four days after the solemn holy day of Yom Kippur, Jews celebrate a seven-day holiday known as Sukkot. Although there is no direct connection to Yom Kippur, Sukkot changes the mood of the fall holiday season.

The basis for Sukkot is biblical: "After the harvest from your threshing floor and your vineyards, you shall celebrate the Feast of Booths for seven days" (Deuteronomy 16:13). In addition, the Bible states: "You shall live in booths seven days in order that future generations may know that I made the Israelite people live in booths when I brought them out of the land of Egypt" (Leviticus 23:42–43).

The holiday of Sukkot celebrates both the conclusion of the fall harvest and commemorates the Jewish people's wandering in the desert after they left Egypt when they lived in temporary tentlike structures—simple booths called *sukkot*.

Today Jews annually build their own sukkot for the week to reexperience that pivotal liberation. In addition to building sukkot, Jews use specified plants to personally thank God for the bounty of the harvest.

Sukkot is a wonderful outdoor holiday filled with symbols and a partylike atmosphere. The mood is festive. The focus of the week's celebration is in the *sukkah* decorated with fruits, vegetables, cornstalks, palms, willows, and other greenery. Family and friends are invited to join us in the sukkah to eat there (weather permitting) and sometimes to even sleep there.

The first day of Sukkot in Reform synagogues and in Israel and the first two days in Conservative and Orthodox synagogues outside of Israel are those that are celebrated as holidays with special rituals within the synagogue. If possible, one should not work or attend school on these days.

GREETINGS

The greeting for Sukkot is *"Hag Sameach*—Happy Holiday." The phrase itself denotes the joy of this festival.

PREPARATIONS FOR SUKKOT

Preparations for Sukkot are detailed. The orientation is not with planning for the holiday meals and guests but with the outdoor setting for the celebration. The first task is to get the sukkah ready.

The Sukkah

The *Mishneh,* the first code of Jewish law, sets certain standards necessary for a functioning sukkah. The sukkah is a rectangular booth with a minimum of three walls. Because a sukkah is a temporary structure, a screened-in porch cannot do. However, an existing trellis can be altered into a sukkah once a year.

The sukkah can be built anywhere outside, in a yard, on a rooftop, in an alleyway, or on an apartment balcony. Because it is built outside, it should be able to withstand the normal flow of wind—even if you live off the bay in San Francisco or the lake in Chicago where the winds can be quite gusty.

At its largest, a household's sukkah should be less than thirty feet long; at its smallest it should fit at least one person, and it should be tall enough for a person to stand comfortably.

The roof of the sukkah is constructed of rafters overlaid with greenery or branches from trees or bushes. The *schach,* as the greenery/branches covering is called, must not be so dense as to prevent the stars from being visible at night, although it must be thick enough to provide shade from the sunlight.

The framework for the sukkah can be made from wood, or plumbing pipe, or even tent poles. The walls of the sukkah are often made from canvas, bamboo shades, colorful bedsheets, or plywood.

For beams to support the sukkah's *schach,* you can use bamboo rods, thin wooden sticks, or even discarded lumber or fallen branches scrounged from your neighborhood. The leafy greens themselves can be gathered from palm fronds or other local greenery.

Some sort of light needs to be brought into the sukkah so that you can see when you eat in the sukkah for the evening meals. There are many ways to accomplish this without being a registered electrician.

If you're not into building a sukkah from scratch yourself, there are kits available from synagogues and other vendors. One such source is Ira Feldman, whose kits come in a variety of sizes and price ranges. He can be reached at P.O. Box 1314, Venice, CA 90294 or (310) 399-7876 and he'll ship the kits anywhere.

In some communities, Jewish youth groups deliver the schach to cover the sukkah roof rafters as a fund-raising project. For years in Los Angeles and Beverly Hills, the palm trees have been trimmed by the city in time for their fronds to be used for the sukkot.

✡

L. A. STORY

A few days before one Sukkot a friend of ours had an "only in L.A." experience. He was driving in an area west of downtown Los Angeles and he spotted some city workers cutting down palm fronds.

He stopped his car and asked if he could have some. The foreperson, an Hispanic woman, told him the fronds were all taken. He asked in amazement, "What do you mean?"

The foreperson looked at him as if he had just arrived from the planet Mars. Then she said, "They're for Sukkos!"

✡

It is also important to plan out the decorations for the sukkah. Simple decorations made from construction paper or paper chains can be fun to hang in the sukkah at a minimal cost. Many people string Rosh Hashanah cards across the walls of the sukkah.

Decorations can get more elaborate: for example, origami designs and animals, special silk-screened posters designed for the sukkah, or even tinted sponge shapes printed on bamboo shades. Some people collect special ornaments to hang in their sukkah year after year, such as Japanese kites or dolls collected from countries all over the world.

Now that the sukkah is built, how is it used? It is a *mitzvah,* a good deed, to eat all the week's meals in the sukkah. And although one is not required to sleep in the sukkah, it can be fun to do so.

(We know of a family who sleeps in the sukkah and has one of those automatic alarm clock/coffeemakers in the sukkah to wake them each morning. For a recent Sukkot, this family built an addition to their sukkah—a separate children's bedroom.)

It is not a requirement to eat in the sukkah if it is raining or snowing. People who live in harsh climates from Rochester, New York, to Seattle, Washington, often quickly rush into the sukkah to say *Kiddush,* the blessing over the wine, while snow or rain is falling, and then run back into the house to eat their meal.

Symbols: The Four Species

Cuttings from four types of plants are used during the holiday as major symbols. Their basis is biblical: "On the first day, you shall take the produce of goodly trees, branches of palm trees, boughs of leafy trees and willows of the brook, and you shall rejoice before the Lord your God, for seven days" (Leviticus 23:40).

These plants are known as the *Arba Minim,* the Four Species. The first species is an etrog, a citron, which looks like a long, slender lemon with a stem on its end. The *pitom,* the elongated stem, makes the etrog kosher, valid for use. The etrog is considered exceptionally beautiful if it is very bumpy. Some say the etrog is a symbol of the seeds of the upcoming harvest year and that a full, beautiful etrog will lead to a fertile future.

The other three plants are bound together. The *lulav*—the palm branch—is woven together with two branches of the *hadas*—the myrtle—and two branches of the *arava*—the willow. All together these three plants are referred to by the name of the largest, the lulav. (When not being used, keep the plants in the refrigerator wrapped in wet paper towels and they will stay fresh during the holiday.)

The meanings of the symbols are endless. Some say they represent different human body parts: the etrog is the heart for compassion; the lulav is the backbone for straight and tall; the hadas is the eye for seeing all; the arava is the mouth for expressing thought and emotion.

A lulav and etrog can be ordered through local synagogues and Jewish organizations—or even by mail. You may contact Bnei Akiva of North America at 25 W. 26th Street, Fourth Floor, New York, NY 10010 or call (212) 889-5260 to order a lulav and etrog. You can also contact Eichler's Bookstore at 1429 Coney Island Ave., Brooklyn, NY 11230 or call (718) 258-7643. Call Eichler's at least two weeks before Sukkot and the lulav and etrog will be sent out next day air so you will get it fresh.

However, if it is possible, a trip to the Lower East Side in Manhattan, Devon Avenue in Chicago, or Fairfax Avenue in Los Angeles brings you close to the experience of how Jews have been buying their lulav and etrog for centuries.

People look for bumps, length, and sweet smells for the etrog, and fresh leaves and a straight branch for the lulav. The experience is taken seriously, and each symbol is examined slowly. And the price? Well, by the time you are settled on your lulav and etrog, it can easily total between $55 and $75 and upward.

The lulav and etrog are used each morning of Sukkot in synagogue (except on Shabbat in Orthodox and some Conservative synagogues). However, even if people do not go to the synagogue, they can recite the blessings and wave the lulav in all directions in their home or sukkah.

SHAKE THAT LULAV!

Here is the specific order of the ritual with which we shake the lulav. This procedure can be done at home, or in the sukkah, or in the synagogue during the morning service before the Hallel psalms.

1. Standing, hold the lulav in your right hand. The long, green stem, called the spine, faces you.
2. Place the etrog in your left hand with its tip—pitom—facing downward.
3. Recite the blessing: Baruch Ata Adonai Elohaynu Melech Haolam, asher keedshanu b'meetzvotav v'tseevanu al netilat lulav. Praised are You Eternal our God, Who makes us holy and Who instructs us to shake the lulav.

4. On the first day of Sukkot in which you shake the lulav, the above blessing is followed with the Shehehayanu blessing: Baruch Ata Adonai Elohaynu Melech Haolam, shehehayanu, v'keeyomanu, v'higeeanu l'zman hazeh.
Praised are You Eternal our God, Who has kept us in life, nurtured us, and allowed us to reach this season.
5. Now move the tip of the etrog facing upward and, still holding the etrog in your left hand and the lulav in your right hand, with your hands held together shake the lulav one time in all directions: north, south, east, west, up, down.

VICKI REIKES FOX

Inviting Guests into the Sukkah

When Jews dwell in the sukkah for the week, they mythically live with their ancestors. In celebrating that linkage, they invite specific ancestors to the sukkah for certain nights. Many people literally sit down to dinner and welcome the biblical matriarchs and patriarchs—Sarah and Abraham, Rebeccah and Isaac, Rachel, Leah, and Jacob. Telling the stories of the honored guests is often part of the celebration.

Sukkot is also a wonderful time to invite friends (Jewish and non-Jewish), family, neighbors, and work associates. It is an informal way to broaden your circle and give others a delightful Jewish experience. You might extend this invitation to those newly arrived in your neighborhood—Soviet and Ethiopian Jews or even new neighbors.

A family in our community annually celebrates with a late-afternoon sukkah party. This outdoor, easy entertaining is an opportunity to welcome old and new friends, adults and children, into the sukkah.

Some people ask their guests to participate in the holiday by bringing homemade decorations for the sukkah or canned foods to be given to a food pantry at a later time.

HOME TRADITIONS

Evening

Two candles are lit at the onset of evening on the first two nights of the holiday. Many people light these candles in the sukkah. But when there is a concern for safety, people light the candles inside their home and then move into the sukkah. Following candle lighting, it is a tradition for parents to bless their children as on Shabbat.

When everyone is gathered together in the sukkah, the holiday Kiddush, the blessing over the wine (or grape juice), is recited. When entering the sukkah to eat for the first time each year, the Shehehayanu prayer is recited at the conclusion of the Kiddush.

The Kiddush is followed by the blessing which acknowledges the privilege of celebrating in the sukkah. The ritual is concluded with the blessing over the *challah,* the sweet round holiday bread, which is then dipped in honey and a piece distributed to each person. After the meal, *Birkat Hamazon,* the prayers of thanksgiving for the food, is sung.

Daytime

A festive meal is served after morning synagogue services. The blessings over the wine, the privilege of sitting in the sukkah, and the challah are recited. The challah is then dipped in honey and a piece given to each person. Birkat Hamazon is again sung to conclude the meal.

POLISH FAMILY SUKKAH

In 1988 I participated with thirty other rabbis in the first Polish Government–sponsored trip to Jewish sites in Poland. My husband's parents both came from Poland, and I was determined to see what remained of their roots there.

So it was with a great deal of excitement that I approached the address on the street in Krakow where my husband's mother grew up in the house that her father had built. The building had been three stories high, with the leather tanning warehouse in the basement and the offices of the very successful tanning business on the first floor. The family had lived on the second and third floors.

Not only was the building there, but the special structure built for the sukkah still remained affixed to the second floor of the building! This sukkah had been built with a removable, hinged roof. During most of the year, the roof would remain in place over the enclosed structure, but for Sukkot the roof would be lifted up and the temporary open roofing would be added. Then the family, protected by the heating inside the room, would sleep under the stars in the harsh climate of a Polish fall.

—K.L.F.

SYNAGOGUE TRADITIONS

The Sukkah

Most synagogues build a large sukkah for the community celebration. Many synagogues will use the sukkah for outdoor evening services or for communal dinners. It is a great way for people to mix and mingle within the synagogue.

Services

The synagogue customs for Sukkot are similar to the other two pilgrimage harvest festivals, Pesach and Shavuot. Specific Torah portions linked to the holiday themes are read in the morning services. The congregation sings *Hallel*, which literally means praise, and is recited on joyous holidays. The Hallel prayer is composed of selections of poetry from Psalms 113 through 118.

On Sukkot, the Hallel psalms are chanted while the etrog and lulav are waved at specific words within the liturgy. Congregants march in circles around the temple with the etrog and lulav in hand. They also chant petitionary prayers which are taken from Psalm 118—"We beseech You, O God, save us, prosper us!"

The In-Between Days

Hol HaMoed, the days of Sukkot following the festival days, are part of the festival. Meals continue in the sukkah as on the first two days of Sukkot. The daily ritual with the lulav and etrog continues throughout the holiday. These intermediate days are those in which people go to school and work.

Shmini Atzeret

Although Shmini Atzeret, the eighth "lingering" day, is commonly considered part of Sukkot proper, it is actually a separate holiday. Shmini Atzeret is a festival in which no work takes place and specific prayers are added to the daily liturgy.

Two candles are lit before sundown at the start of this holiday. Following this, one *Yizkor* candle is lit in memory of each close relative who has died. (There is no blessing that accompanies the lighting of this special candle.) The festive meal is begun with Kiddush and the other blessings and concluded with Birkat Hamazon as on Sukkot.

The following morning in synagogue the Yizkor service is recited. During Yizkor Jews remember both their deceased loved ones and martyrs of the Jewish people. In addition, Shmini Atzeret is the holiday in which Jews begin to recite the prayer for rain—to coincide with the growing season in Israel—praising God for "making the wind to blow and the rain to fall" (*The Traditional Prayer Book,* edited and translated by David De Sola Pool, New York: Behrman House, Inc., 1960, p. 382).

After morning services, the rituals for the holiday meal are the same as for Sukkot.

INSIGHTS

Names of the Holiday

Sukkot, known by various names that highlight different aspects of its liturgical themes, is considered the third of the pilgrimage festivals, festivals which recall the time when people came to Jerusalem with the finest produce from their harvest.

Sukkot is known as *HeHag,* "the Festival," for it was the most important of the pilgrimage festivals. Sukkot is also called *Hag HaAsif,* "the Feast of the Gathering of the Harvest."

Sukkot is referred to as *Hag Adonai,* "God's Festival." It was interpreted that within the holiday Jews experience God's nurturance and gift of freedom; therefore, it was seen as God's festival.

In addition, Sukkot is known by a fourth name, *Zman Simchateynu,* "the Season of Our Rejoicing," the time in which Jews rejoice in their liberation from Egyptian bondage.

The Sukkah

Consider the simplicity of the sukkah. It is natural, temporary, even a bit inconvenient. We may learn that the best things in life are fragile and often relatively short-lived. We can explore ways in which we can emphasize this concept. How can we demonstrate that what we cannot see but that which we feel is the best in life? How can we show love between generations and care for the world as a whole? What concrete things can we do to reaffirm values emphasizing that people are more important than the collecting of things?

The Reading of the Book of Ecclesiastes

Kohelet, the Book of Ecclesiastes, is read on the Shabbat morning that falls during the week of Sukkot. According to modern scholarship, the name Kohelet may be understood as the "gatherer" of popular sayings. Therefore, the book can be seen as a collection of wisdom gathered from the people and later compiled by an editor. Some traditionalists say that the author is King Solomon; he supposedly wrote Kohelet near the end of his life.

The book of Kohelet is rich in its exploration of the meanings of life. It is surprisingly modern in its insights, bothersome in its truths. It emphasizes human limits and accepts those as such. "There is a season set for everything, a time for every experience under heaven" (Ecclesiastes 3:1).

There is an acceptance of the time and place for winning and losing, for love and hate, for birth and death. There is an acceptance of the reality that God determines the times and places for significant human events.

There is also skepticism, as Kohelet speaks of the gathering of his wealth: "I got enjoyment from my wealth. And that was all I got out of my wealth" (Ecclesiastes

2:10). There is a resigned reality that this is the way it is: "There is nothing new beneath the sun" (Ecclesiastes 1:9).

There is a subtle bitterness in the recognition that the pursuit of power in life does not matter. Rather, Kohelet says, "Vanity, vanity, all is air—vapor—vanity."

Kohelet is linked to Sukkot because Jews pose the questions that Kohelet does as they sit and reflect in the sukkah. They see friends, food, palm fronds, fruits and vegetables. Kohelet reflects on life, on its limits, on its benefits. All are here, in the sukkah and on earth, for a short time only.

How do we understand these quick endings and new beginnings? How do we decorate our lives with "greenery"? How does adding natural beauty enhance the meaning in our lives? What are our feelings about our own striving for money and success? These are the questions we can explore as we discuss Kohelet.

ACTIVITIES

1. Your neighborhood may enjoy an activity that is found in our community. We organize a progressive lunch sukkah walk in the neighborhood. Each family provides a bit of the meal while we go from sukkah to sukkah. People talk and enjoy the different styles and decorations found in the various sukkot.

Our neighborhood sukkah walk is getting so large that we are considering ways to change it in order to accommodate more families each year. One suggestion for next year is that, instead of serving food in each sukkah to upwards of fifty people, the host family at each sukkah will tell a story for Sukkot or put on a short skit or perform a song. In this way we can invite all our neighborhood into our sukkah without worrying about the logistics of feeding everyone!

2. Opportunities for parent-child interactions are many during Sukkot.

a. Of course, building a sukkah together is perhaps the best activity for this holiday. Planning for the building of the sukkah, and especially its decorating, involves the whole household in a fun-filled set of activities. Artistic decorations are always appreciated. Make harvest scenes, as well as artificial, brightly colored vegetables and plants to decorate the sukkah!

But even if you do not build a sukkah, you can build a mini-shoebox sukkah. Decorate it with construction paper, leaves, Popsicle sticks, doll furniture and dolls.

b. Foods for the holiday are those which utilize the fall harvest. Stuffed cabbage—cabbage leaves stuffed with ground meat or a form of grain—is one traditional food. You'll find recipes for this on pp. 69–71.

c. After the week of Sukkot the sukkah's greenery turns brown and withers and company is no longer invited. This is a natural and stress-free opportunity in which parents and children can share learning about beginnings and endings, birth and death.

Two books for adults to read together with children on this topic are: *Dusty Was My Friend: Coming to Terms with Loss* by Andrea Clardy (New York: Human Service Press, 1984); *About Dying: An Open Family Book for Parents and Children Together* by Sara Bonnett Stein (New York: Walker & Company, 1974).

d. And on Sukkot, when Jews welcome their revered matriarchs, patriarchs, and other honored guests into the sukkah, it is a fitting time to consider looking for roots. Make a chart of your own family. Include their Jewish names, birth and death dates, country of origin, and other interesting family facts.

SEARCHING FOR ROOTS

On a family summer vacation trip to Washington, D.C., in 1991 we braved the heat to visit the National Archives and utilize the indexes for United States immigration records to look for traces of my husband's grandfather, Jacob Miller. The only two things that are known about his roots are: The original family name was probably Maduke (or Menduke) and the family descended from the Cohanim, the ancient Temple priests in Jerusalem.

Needless to say, the list of Jacob Millers immigrating to the port of New York (immigration records are indexed by port of entry) in the early years of this century were endless. Frustrated, I turned to the 1910 census records for Philadelphia, even though I wasn't sure Jacob Miller was in Philadelphia by 1910.

I am convinced that I may have found the correct Jacob Miller. The clues are consistent with the recorded information: He lived with a cousin whose last name was Cohen (obviously a Cohen as he himself was) and another uncle,

aunt, and cousin Seider. He was about the right age for the Jacob Miller who came as a teenager without his parents and then enlisted in the Jewish Legion in World War I.

Now that the census records provided me with the year that this Jacob Miller immigrated—1907—in future research I can go back to immigration records for that year for ships entering the ports of New York and Philadelphia and try to find him. And what can I find?

Starting in 1907 the immigration records had twenty-nine columns of useful personal information which may offer clues as to whether this is the correct Jacob Miller. The most tantalizing facet is that, since I learned that the records were normally prepared in the port of departure or on board ship (before people got their "Ellis Island" names), I may be able to actually trace the original family name in Russia. I will be able to use the Soundex system—devised to eliminate confusion over various spellings of a name—to look for Yaakov Maduke or Menduke.

I also read the booklet "They Came in Ships" by John P. Colletta (Salt Lake City: Ancestry Publishing, Inc., 1989). This booklet, available from the National Archives gift shop and the publisher (801-531-1790), instructs would-be family researchers on utilizing resources in the National Archives.

You can call the National Archives in Washington, D.C., to learn which of the eleven regional archives is closest to you. Call that archives and ask to be sent the booklet describing the genealogical information available in your regional archives. You may find the information you seek is closer than Washington, D.C.

Once you have all the information you can find, there are many ways to utilize this material. You can even make your own family tree and hang it in your sukkah each year.

So happy searching! The information you find may be your own!

—P.Z.M.

RECIPES

The rule of thumb for Sukkot is "Keep It Simple." Because you will be eating outside, on paper and plastic, in warm or cold weather, consider what will be comfortable to eat in those surroundings.

TRADITIONAL STUFFED CABBAGE

2 lbs. ground chuck or ground turkey or ground veal
1 c. of bread crumbs or ½ c. cooked rice
2 beaten eggs with a little water added
1 tsp. salt
1 small onion, chopped
pepper
garlic powder
whole head of green cabbage
1 large onion, sliced

Mix all ingredients, except cabbage and large sliced onion, together. Form oval balls from about ½ c. of mixture each. Roll in cabbage leaves which have been softened in boiling water or steamed (see TIPS on p. 70). Place large sliced onion in bottom of roasting pan. Place wrapped meat on top on onions.

SAUCE:

2 c. of canned tomatoes

2 Tbsp. of sugar (brown or white)

⅛ tsp. baking soda

2 Tbsp. of vinegar or 2 Tbsp. lemon juice
or ⅔ tsp. sour salt

½ tsp. table salt

Mix sauce ingredients and pour sauce over wrapped meat. On top of sauce, spread ½ lb. of prunes with pits. (Remove pits before serving.)

Bake covered in 300-degree oven for 2 hours. Then gently turn over cabbage rolls and bake for additional 30 minutes uncovered. Finally, turn cabbage rolls back and bake uncovered for additional 30 minutes (3 hours in all).

TIPS: 1) Instead of boiling or steaming cabbage, it can be put in freezer for a short time and then thawed. Then the leaves will be pliable enough not to require steaming or boiling. 2) In wrapping the meatballs in cabbage, wrap as if putting a baby into a receiving blanket, then tuck remaining flap in pocket.

QUICK CABBAGE CASSEROLE

3 lbs. of ground chuck or ground turkey or
ground veal

3 beaten eggs with a little water added

1 c. of Minute Rice, uncooked

1½ tsp. table salt

¼ tsp. pepper

garlic powder

1 medium onion, chopped

3 Tbsp. water

3 Tbsp. ketchup

1 tsp. of prepared mustard

whole head of green cabbage

1 tsp. coarse kosher salt

Mix all ingredients, except cabbage and coarse salt, together. Form oval balls from about ½ c. of mixture each.

SAUCE:

1 can or carton Ocean Spray cranberry
sauce

1 can or carton Ocean Spray
raspberry-cranberry sauce

1 large jar of marinara sauce

Heat the combined sauce. Place in baking pan. Place meatballs in hot sauce.

Cut head of cabbage into quarters. Wash quarter thoroughly and shred ¼ head over the meat and sauce. Sprinkle ¼ tsp. of kosher salt over the cabbage. Repeat process, forming layers of cabbage and kosher salt, until cabbage is used up. Bake covered in 300-degree oven for 2 hours. (Cabbage will sink to bottom.)

SUKKOT BLESSINGS

Introductory meditation to be recited together before candle lighting:

In ancient times Jews celebrated this harvest festival by traveling to Jerusalem. There they gathered at the Temple to build sukkot and offer fruit and grains in thanksgiving for the bounty of the natural world.

Today we gather to thank God for all the goodness in our lives, for the beauty of nature, for the love we feel for one another, for the Sukkot tradition which we share. May our celebration increase our awareness of your ongoing gifts, O God.

Candle lighting:

(Recite this blessing, then light the candles. If it is Shabbat, light the candles first and then recite the blessing.)

Baruch Ata Adonai Elohaynu Melech Haolam, asher keedshanu b'mitzvotav v'tzivanu l'hadleek ner shel (Shabbat v') Yom Tov.
Blessed are You Adonai, Eternal One, Who enables us to welcome (Shabbat and) Sukkot by kindling these lights.

Shehehayanu:

(On the first night of Sukkot add:)

Baruch Ata Adonai Elohaymu Melech Haolam, shehehayanu, v'keeyomanu v'higeeyanu laz'man hazeh.
Blessed are You Adonai, Eternal One, Who has kept us alive, sustained us, and encouraged us to celebrate this joyful festival.

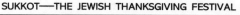

Parents' blessing for their children:
   (Place hands on children and recite.)

FOR BOYS:
May God touch you as you strive to live in the image of Ephraim and Menasshe, leaders who carried on our traditions with pride.

FOR GIRLS:
May God touch you as you strive to live in the image of Sarah and Rebeccah, Rachel and Leah, leaders who carried on our traditions with pride.

CONTINUE SAYING FOR BOTH:
May the Eternal bless you and keep you.
May the Eternal bring you warmth and protect you.
May the Eternal embrace you and grant you peace. Amen.

Sukkot Evening Kiddush:
   (Raise wine cups and recite. Then drink the wine.)

We praise God with this symbol of fullness, and give thanks for the opportunities we have to share life's blessings.

Baruch Ata Adonai Elohaynu Melech Haolam, boray p'ree hagafen.
Blessed are You Adonai, Eternal One, Who creates fruit from the vine.

Baruch Ata Adonai Elohaynu Melech Haolam, asher bachar banu meekol ahm, v'romemanu meekol lashon, v'keedshanu b'meetzvotav. V'teetayn lanu, Adonai Elohaynu, b'ahavah (Shabbatot leemnucha oo) moadeem l'seemcha, chageem u'z-maneem l'sasson et yom (haShabbat hazeh v'et) yom hag haSukkot hazeh, z'man seemchataynu, mikrah kodesh zaycher l'tzeeat meetzrayim. Kee banu bacharta v'otanu keedashta meekol ha-ahmeem, (v'Shabbat) oo'moaday kodshecha (b'ahavah oo'vratzon) b'seemcha oo'vsasson heenhaltanu. Baruch Ata Adonai M'kadesh (ha-Shabbat v') Yisrael, v'hazmaneem.

Blessed are You Adonai, Eternal One, Who has chosen us from among all people, sanctified us with holy acts, and given special times and seasons for rejoicing. (Shabbat and) Sukkot remind us of the times for celebration, recalling the exodus from

Egypt. You have distinguished us from all people, and have given us (the Shabbat and) holy festivals full of joy and inspiration. Blessed are You Adonai, Eternal One, Who sanctifies (the Shabbat,) the people Israel, and our sacred seasons.

Shehehayanu:
> (On the first night of Sukkot add:)

Baruch Ata Adonai Elohaynu Melech Haolam, shehehayanu, v'keeyomanu v'higeeyanu laz'man hazeh.
Blessed are You Adonai, Eternal One, Who has kept us alive, sustained us, and encouraged us to celebrate this joyful festival.

Shmini Atzeret Evening Kiddush:
> (Raise wine cups and recite. Then drink the wine.)

We praise God with this symbol of fullness, and give thanks for the opportunities we have to share life's blessings.

Baruch Ata Adonai Elohaynu Melech Haolam, boray p'ree hagafen.
Blessed are You Adonai, Eternal One, Who creates fruit from the vine.

Baruch Ata Adonai Elohaynu Melech Haolam, asher bachar banu meekol ahm, v'romemanu meekol lashon, v'keedshanu b'meetzvotav. V'teetayn lanu, Adonai Elohaynu, b'ahavah (Shabbatot leemnucha oo) moadeem l'seemcha, chageem u'z-maneem l'sasson et yom (haShabbat hazeh v'et) Yom Shmini, hag haatzeret hazeh, z'man simchataynu, mikrah kodesh zaycher l'tzeeat meetzrayim. Kee banu bacharta v'otanu keedashta meekol ha-ahmeem, (v'Shabbat) oo'moaday kodshecha (b'ahavah oo'vratzon) b'seemcha oo'vsasson heenhaltanu). Baruch Ata Adonai M'kadesh (ha-Shabbat v') Yisrael, v'hazmaneem.

Blessed are You Adonai, Eternal One, Who has chosen us from among all people, sanctified us with holy acts, and given special times and seasons for rejoicing. (Shabbat and) Shmini Atzeret remind us of the times for celebration, recalling the exodus from Egypt. You have distinguished us from all people, and have given us (the Shabbat and) holy festivals full of joy and inspiration. Blessed are You Adonai, Eternal One, Who sanctifies (the Shabbat,) the people Israel, and our sacred seasons.

Shehehayanu:

Baruch Ata Adonai Elohaynu Melech Haolam, shehehayanu, v'keeyomanu v'higeeyanu laz'man hazeh.

Blessed are You Adonai, Eternal One, Who has kept us alive, sustained us, and encouraged us to celebrate this joyful festival.

Daytime Kiddush for Sukkot and Shmini Atzeret:

(Raise wine cups and recite. Then drink the wine.)

El Moaday Adonai Meekrah-ay kodesh, asher teekrehoo otam b'moadam. VayDaber Moshe et moaday Adonai el b'nay Yisrael.

These are the sacred times appointed by God; and you shall announce them in their season.

Baruch Ata Adonai Elohaynu Melech Haolam, boray p'ree hagafen.

Blessed are You Adonai, Eternal One, Who creates fruit from the vine.

Blessing for sitting in the sukkah:

Baruch Ata Adonai Elohaynu Melech Haolam, asher keedshanu b'meetzvotav v'tzeevanu layshayv b'sukkah.

Blessed are You Adonai, Eternal One, Who brought us out of Egypt to sit freely under the sukkah.

Blessing over the challah:

(Remove challah cover and recite. After blessing, dip challah in honey and distribute a piece to each person.)

Baruch Ata Adonai Elohaynu Melech Haolam, hamotzi lechem meen ha-aretz.

Blessed are You Adonai, Eternal One, Who creates bread from the earth.

5
SIMCHAT TORAH—DANCING
IN FULL CIRCLE

WHILE the holiday of Simchat Torah coincides with the conclusion of Sukkot, it is truly its own holiday. On Simchat Torah the annual cycle of reading the *Torah,* the first five books of the Hebrew Bible, is completed and immediately begun again. This one-day holiday is celebrated by dancing with the scrolls of the Torah—physically demonstrating the link between Torah and the Jewish people.

The Torah is the central symbol of Judaism. The Hebrew Bible contains the traditions, history, and laws of the Jewish people. Its stories and values are transmitted from generation to generation. Today the text of the Torah is available from many different publishing houses in a myriad of languages.

Each physical Torah scroll is handwritten on pieces of parchment. The individual pieces are sewn together to create a very long scroll containing the entire first five books of the Hebrew Bible. The scrolled Torah is covered with an outer covering of decorated fine material and adorned with silver or, in Sephardic practice, enclosed in a silver or wooden case.

Whether Jews dance with the scrolls of the Torah on the streets of Moscow or in the synagogue in Hattiesburg, Mississippi, they are showing pride in their Jewish identity. The Torah itself may be heavy to carry, but the celebration marks an unencumbered joy that Jewish people are free to participate in this moment each year.

When we dance with the Torah we experience a sense of personal connectedness to it. The Torah did not only belong to our ancestors, but it belongs to us today—to women and men—to cherish it, study it, and dance with it.

The Torah is made up of the books of *B'raisheet*—Genesis; *Sh'mot*—Exodus; *Va'yikra*—Leviticus; *Bmidbar*—Numbers; and *Dvarim*—Deuteronomy. The Torah is central to the Jewish people because it contains laws and traditions, customs and celebrations. It also reveals the ongoing narrative that is the history and culture of the Jewish people.

Simchat Torah is a holiday not found either in biblical or in later Talmudic sources. It was created while the Jewish people were in exile in Babylonia to affirm their dedication to the Torah even while they were away from their homeland.

On this holiday people rest at home and in the synagogue and, if possible, do not go to work or school.

GREETINGS

The greeting for this holiday is *"Hag Sameach*—Happy Holiday."

HOME TRADITIONS

Evening

The holiday is welcomed, as is customary with festivals, by the lighting of two candles at the onset of evening. Following candle lighting, it is a tradition for parents to bless their children.

The festive evening meal is eaten in the home, not the *sukkah*. At the beginning of the meal, Jews recite *Kiddush*, the blessing over the wine (or grape juice), and continue with the blessing over the *challah,* which is dipped in honey and given to each person. The *Birkat Hamazon,* the thanksgiving blessing, is sung at the conclusion of the meal.

Daytime

After morning services a festive meal is served. The blessings over the wine and the challah are recited prior to the meal. This is the last time in the fall holiday season in which challah is dipped in honey. The Birkat Hamazon is sung at the conclusion of the meal. People rest and relax throughout the afternoon.

SYNAGOGUE TRADITIONS

Evening Service

The most popular aspects of Simchat Torah occur in the synagogue at evening services. After the initial prayers are recited, the focus of the synagogue celebration begins with the recitation of praises to God and the Torah.

Various members of the community are asked to read a verse in the prayerbook, then the congregation responds. This honor of reading often goes to the oldest members, community leaders, new arrivals from foreign countries, benefactors of the synagogue, its teachers, or its rabbis.

The evening service begins when the Ark containing the Torah scrolls is opened. All congregants rise as the Torahs are lifted from the Ark. It is an honor to carry a Torah, and again various leaders and representatives are usually honored first. However, each Jew should carry a Torah on this occasion, so throughout the evening the Torahs are passed from person to person.

The leaders sing and carry the Torah, followed by a procession of congregants, young and old, men and women, who sing and dance. The procession encircles the synagogue, and each procession is called a *hakafah,* or circuit.

When the seventh cyclical procession is completed, all Torahs but one are returned to the Ark. The leader then continues the evening service with the prayers for removing the Torah from the Ark.

It is only recently in American Reform and Conservative congregations that women have been allowed to carry a Torah. Some women still hesitate to hold a sacred scroll. Some claim they cannot put down their children to pick up the Torah.

Yet it is vitally important for our children to see both women and men, their mothers and fathers, actively participating in their heritage. So encourage everyone to pass their children to another adult, pick up a Torah, and celebrate!

Children themselves participate through dance, song, and, of course, by carrying apples on top of Israeli flags. Why apples? We can only answer, "It's a tradition." (The apple may represent sweetness and knowledge gained through the study of and relationship to Torah.) In congregations that have very light, little Torahs or other small sacred scrolls, children are often allowed to carry these scrolls.

The Torah reading is taken from the very end of the fifth book, Deuteronomy, and then from the very beginning of the first book, Genesis. This signifies that there are no endings to the Torah process because study and learning never cease.

Morning Service

The morning Simchat Torah service is similar to other morning holiday services with special emphasis given to *Hallel,* the special holiday psalms. After the singing of Hallel, seven hakafot begin again. After the hakafot the Torah is read.

The reader recites this same concluding Torah portion (Deuteronomy 33:1–26) over and over again until every member of the community has had an *aliyah*—an opportunity to be called up to recite the blessings over the Torah.

Some congregations will call people up by groups. Sometimes this is done humorously, calling all people over forty, all whose children require braces, all accountants, schoolteachers, and so on.

After all adults have had an aliyah (in traditional synagogues this does not include women), all children are called up for the aliyah called *kol hanearim*—the voice of all the children. This is the only time in the year that children are called to the Torah prior to their *Bar/Bat Mitzvah*. It is wonderful to see so many young faces singing the blessings as a *tallit,* a large prayer shawl, is held high above them.

INSIGHTS

Centrality of the Torah to the Jewish People

Many times in Jewish history Jews were expelled from the lands in which they lived. We think of the ancient expulsion from Israel to Babylonia, the fifteenth-century expulsion from Spain into Poland and Amsterdam, the modern-day expulsion from Germany, Austria, and Poland to America. However, after the first expulsion, Jews were never again a land-based people. They developed professions that did not require ownership of land for agriculture or land for real estate development. They were and are a mobile people.

What Jews took with them at each expulsion were values, traditions, and beliefs. These are contained in the Torah, which give the Jewish people a unique destiny. The Torah and its demands for certain behaviors in family life and communal life allowed Jews to reestablish themselves after each forced uprooting. The Torah gave them the hope needed to believe that life would be better in a new land. The centrality of the Torah as a guide and inspiration kept them alive.

The Political Import

Simchat Torah has been understood in modern times to carry a political message to the Jews in oppressed countries. During the communist reign in the Soviet Union, when only the Jewish elderly dared to go to synagogue, Simchat Torah was the one holiday in which Jews of all ages would gather at the synagogue, to see and be seen by other Jews celebrating their holiday.

Moving descriptions of Simchat Torah celebrations worldwide can be found in such stories as "Moscow via the Eyes of Eli Wiesel" and "The Night of Hakafot" by Shalom Aleichem (Philip Goodman, *The Hanukkah Anthology,* Philadelphia: Jewish Publication Society, 1976, pp. 204 and 281).

The Torah: All Knowledge Is Contained Within It

A traditional phrase that refers to Torah states: "Turn, turn, turn it: all is within the Torah." This indicates the vast levels of wisdom that are to be found within the biblical tradition. The phrase highlights the variety of knowledge that Jews have attributed to the Torah, including history, law, literature, and folktales.

But on an even deeper level, aspects of human relationships found in the Torah speak to us today. The Torah focuses on family struggles such as sibling rivalry, separation anxiety, and marital conflict. The Torah emphasizes that growth and change are difficult for individuals and for nations. Even as individuals, we, too, can say "turn, turn, turn it; all knowledge is within the Torah."

Unmitigated Joy at Dancing with Torah

The frenzy of activity and joy found at Simchat Torah is similar to that at Jewish weddings. The music begins, the Torah comes out of the Ark. Initially the march is slow and careful, but then the music speeds up. The line dancers wind in and around those carrying the Torah. As the music changes, the direction of dancing suddenly shifts. But care is taken to encircle the Torah, ensuring it is the center of attention.

For many people this is one of the few times during the year that happiness can be so freewheeling. Certainly, in the Orthodox community, this is one of the few times of the year to let excitement and fervor encircle the community. It is a time to loosen certain restraints of serious synagogue behavior.

However, even in those settings the rules separating Orthodox men and women in the synagogue are still maintained; only the men dance with the Torah, while the women dance on their side of the synagogue. In more liberal Conservative and Reform synagogues, men and women dance together with the Torah.

Simchat Torah enables adults to demonstrate to the next generation by actions, not only by words, how central the Torah is to their lives. The unbroken cycle of the year of Torah can bring joy to each and every Jewish community throughout the world.

So wear comfortable shoes—and may joy dance into your souls!

EVERYONE IS WELCOME!

One of the wonderful facets of this holiday is that anyone can walk into a synagogue for Simchat Torah and participate in the circle dancing that weaves in and out around the people holding and dancing with the Torahs. If you don't know the words to the Hebrew songs, just hum along. And if you don't know the dance steps, just move your feet in time to the music as you're pulled along by the person in front of you and pushed by the person behind you.

The circle of dancers snakes around and around, with dancers breaking in all the time to join hands, while others, tired from their exertions, drop out. Frequently refreshments are available to reward the celebrants. Children wave their flags and munch on their apples. Old and young alike join together in this powerful expression of Judaism.

You've got to see it to believe it and feel it! Come dance next year!

ACTIVITIES

1. Because Simchat Torah follows immediately after Sukkot, crafts for Simchat Torah can be made during Sukkot week.

a. It is traditional to make flags that can be carried in the Torah processional.

Take a 2′ × 3′ piece of sturdy paper and glue or tape the narrow end to a ruler or dowel. Decorate on both sides with freehand drawings, paintings, papercuts, or stencil designs.

The flags can also be made from cloth, using tie-dye or stitchery for the decorations. Wrap the cloth around cardboard. Attach to ruler or dowel and hold it high!

b. It is also fun to create Torah scrolls. Take sheets of parchment and illustrate the stories from the Bible. Attach the separate illustrations to each other, then attach each end of the scroll to dowels. Roll the two sides toward each other. Wrap a cloth tie around your scroll and carry it throughout the synagogue.

c. You might enjoy creating artistic poster expressions of Torah scenes that are symbolic of family names or favorite biblical tales. These posters can be mounted and carried in the procession.

d. The first chapter of the book of Genesis deals with the creation of the world: "In the beginning God created the heaven and the earth." The description of the six "days" of creation can be quite exciting to children and can be incorporated into art projects for various age groups that can be done in preparation for the holiday.

One such project is to create a mural that depicts the creation of the world beginning with day one and progressing to day six. Children can color or paint the mural or can cut out magazine pictures or other existing material in order to make a collage of the six "days" of creation.

2. Another wonderful activity can be to learn how a Torah scroll is made. Visit a Jewish scribe and learn about the process, the time, and materials that are used to make a Torah. You can read the book *A Torah is Written* by Paul Cowan (Philadelphia: Jewish Publication Society, 1986) to prepare for the visit.

3. A fun-learning activity for children is to participate in a Torah "roll" at a synagogue. The Torah is unfurled on several contiguous tables and the children are allowed to view the parchment sections that are stitched together and study some of the finer points of the handwritten scroll. A leader can describe how to recognize the visual forms of certain sections of the Torah: poetry is set out in a wide, open style, empty space is found between different sections of the Torah, and so on.

4. Consider enrolling in a Torah study group—or any other ongoing adult Jewish study. Call the temples or Jewish centers in your city to locate current courses. Or start your own—even a lunch-time study group at work.

RECIPES

TZIMMES

3 carrots (or more) (peeled)
4 sweet potatoes (peeled)
3 tart apples
½ cup brown sugar

3 Tbsp. margarine
1 cup water
1 6-oz. package dried apricots
cinnamon, optional

Cook carrots and potatoes in water until soft. Drain liquid and slice. Pare and slice apples. Alternate layers of carrots, apples, and potatoes with the brown sugar, margarine, apricots, and cinnamon. Add water, cover, and bake in 350-degree oven for 1 hour (or until apples are soft). Baste with its own juice occasionally. Remove cover for last 15 minutes to brown top. Serves 6.

SIMCHAT TORAH BLESSINGS

Introductory meditation to be recited before candle lighting:

Today we gather to thank God for all the goodness in our lives, for the beauty of nature, for the love we feel for one another, for the Simchat Torah tradition which we share.

May our celebration increase our awareness of your ongoing gifts, O God.

Candle lighting:
    (Recite this blessing, then light the candles. If it is Shabbat, light the candles first, then recite the blessing.)

Baruch Ata Adonai Elohaynu Melech Haolam, asher keedshanu b'mitzvotav v'tzivanu l'hadleek ner shel (Shabbat v') Yom Tov.
Blessed are You Adonai, Eternal One, Who enables us to welcome (Shabbat and) Simchat Torah by kindling these lights.

Shehehayanu:
Baruch Ata Adonai Elohaynu Melech Haolam, shehehayanu, v'keeyomanu v'higeeyanu laz'man hazeh.
Blessed are You Adonai, Eternal One, Who has kept us alive, sustained us, and encouraged us to celebrate this joyful festival.

Parents' blessing for their children:
    (Place hands on children and recite.)

FOR BOYS:

May God touch you as you strive to live in the image of Ephraim and Menasshe, leaders who carried on our traditions with pride.

FOR GIRLS:

May God touch you as you strive to live in the image of Sarah and Rebeccah, Rachel and Leah, leaders who carried on our traditions with pride.

CONTINUE SAYING FOR BOTH:

May the Eternal bless you and keep you.
May the Eternal bring you warmth and protect you.
May the Eternal embrace you and grant you peace. Amen.

Evening Kiddush:
(Raise wine cups and recite. Then drink the wine.)

We praise God with this symbol of fullness, and give thanks for the opportunities we have to share life's blessings.

Baruch Ata Adonai Elohaynu Melech Haolam, boray p'ree hagafen.
Blessed are You Adonai, Eternal One, Who creates fruit from the vine.

Baruch Ata Adonai Elohaynu Melech Haolam, asher bachar banu meekol ahm, v'romemanu meekol lashon, v'keedshanu b'meetzvotav. V'teetayn lanu, Adonai Elohaynu, b'ahavah (Shabbatot leemnucha oo) moadeem l'seemcha, chageem u'z-maneem l'sasson et yom (haShabbat hazeh v'et) yom hag haatzeret hazeh, z'man seemchataynu, mikrah kodesh zaycher l'tzeeat meetzrayim. Kee banu bacharta v'otanu keedashta meekol ha-ahmeem, (v'Shabbat) oo'moaday kodshecha (b'ahavah oo'vratzon) b'seemcha oo'vsasson hee-haltanu. Baruch Ata Adonai M'kadesh (ha-Shabbat v') Yisrael v'hazmaneem.

Blessed are You Adonai, Eternal One, Who has chosen us from among all people, sanctified us with holy acts, and given special times and seasons for rejoicing. (Shabbat and) Simchat Torah remind us of the times for celebration, recalling the exodus from Egypt and the gift of Torah. You have distinguished us from all people, and have given us (the Shabbat and) holy festivals full of joy and inspiration. Blessed are You

Adonai, Eternal One, Who sanctifies (the Shabbat,) the people Israel, and our sacred seasons.

Shehehayanu:
Baruch Ata Adonai Elohaynu Melech Haolam, shehehayanu, v'keeyomanu v'higeeyanu laz'man hazeh.
Blessed are You Adonai, Eternal One, Who has kept us alive, sustained us, and encouraged us to celebrate this joyful festival.

Daytime Kiddush:
(Raise wine cups and recite. Then drink the wine.)

El Moaday Adonai Meekrah-ay kodesh, asher teekrehoo otam b'moadam. VayDaber Moshe et moaday Adonai el b'nay Yisrael.
These are the sacred times appointed by God; and you shall announce them in their season.

Baruch Ata Adonai Elohaynu Melech Haolam, boray p'ree hagafen.
Blessed are You Adonai, Eternal One, Who creates fruit from the vine.

Blessing over the challah:
(Remove challah cover and recite. After blessing, dip challah in honey and distribute pieces to each person.)

Baruch Ata Adonai Elohaynu Melech Haolam, hamotzi lechem meen ha-aretz.
Blessed are You Adonai, Eternal One, Who creates bread from the earth.

6
HANUKKAH—
CELEBRATE WITH LIGHTS

Hanukkah, O Hanukkah, come light the menorah.
Let's have a party, we'll all dance the horah.
Gather 'round the table, we'll give you a treat.
Dreidels to play with and latkes to eat.

THIS popular Hanukkah song captures the spirit of this fun winter festival, which occurs between late November and late December. Its eight nights and days are filled with song, stories, games, and foods. Hanukkah is the time to light the *menorah*—a nine-branched candelabrum, to play with *dreidels*—four-sided tops, and to eat *latkes*—fried potato pancakes.

Hanukkah honors an historical event—the struggle for religious freedom. Hanukkah commemorates a time when the ancient homeland of the Jews—now known as Israel—was ruled by the Greeks in the second century before the common era. The Greeks threatened to eliminate the religious faith and customs of the Jewish people.

A small band of Jews resolved to forfeit their lives if necessary to preserve their heritage. Their successful struggle against overwhelming odds determined that the Jewish people and their unique beliefs and practices would survive.

Today Hanukkah—meaning rededication—emphasizes an annual rededication to Jewish heritage. Jews pledge themselves anew to their beliefs and practices. This is done by lighting the Hanukkah candles or oil lamps and by living with Jewish pride. These actions "publicize the miracle of rededication" and demonstrate the themes of Hanukkah.

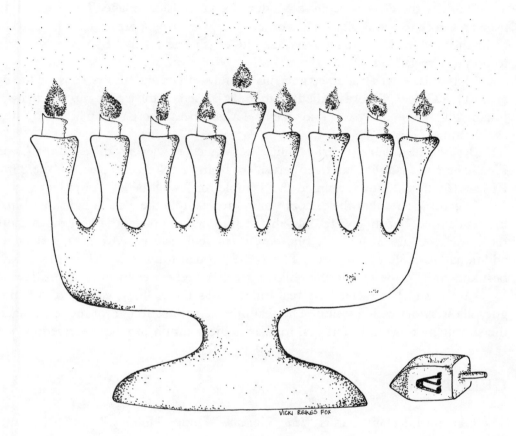

VICKI REIKES FOX

THE STORY OF HANUKKAH

In the year 167 B.C.E. (before the common era), the Greek king Antiochus Epiphanes forced all the people under his rule to adopt Greek culture in the land we know today as the State of Israel. Some Jews were intrigued by Greek culture and wanted to assimilate aspects of that external culture into their own lives. These Jews were attracted to Greek life, its gods, its emphasis on beauty and a powerful body.

Other Jews were abhorred by the price of this demand: Among other Jewish practices outlawed, the observance of Shabbat and circumcision of eight-day-old boys were forbidden. In addition, the worship of Greek gods and other atrocities took place in the Temple, the center of Jewish ritual observance, in the holy city of Jerusalem.

One day the Greeks came to Modin, a small hillside village. There they established a Greek religious altar. They ordered Jews to bring a pig as a sacrifice to show obedience to Greek rule. Mattathias, an old Jewish priest, killed a Jew who was about to do the Greeks' bidding.

Mattathias's action sparked guerrilla warfare and he and his five sons led the fight against the Greeks. Before he died, Mattathias passed on the leadership role to his son Judah. The Jewish army was known as the Maccabees, those men who were "strong as a hammer."

Because of Judah's superior military strategies, he cleverly defeated the Greeks. Finally he and his followers freed Jerusalem from Greek rule. There, on the 25th of Kislev, 165 B.C.E., they reclaimed the Temple for Jewish belief and practice.

Legend asserts that the victors wanted to rekindle the eternal light that burned in the Temple, but they were only able to find one unopened flask of oil. Although there was enough oil for only one day, it miraculously lasted for eight days until additional oil could be prepared. This is the popular miracle for which Hanukkah is best known, and the reason the holiday is celebrated for eight miraculous days.

And the real miracle? The real miracle was the military victory of a band of guerrilla warriors with a vision. The real miracle is the strength of the lesser against the seemingly powerful. The real miracle is the triumph of religious freedom.

GREETINGS

The greeting for Hanukkah is *"Hag Sameach*—Happy Holiday."

HOME TRADITIONS

Menorahs

The central symbol for Hanukkah is light. This image is found in the earliest Jewish source for Hanukkah in the Talmud, the codification of Jewish law and customs from the second through sixth centuries, in a discussion asking: "What is Hanukkah?" The rabbis' response focused on the oil found in the desecrated Temple. Although that vat contained only enough oil to last one day, it lasted eight days.

Why is *this* miracle emphasized? The rabbis wanted to stress the miracle of the oil and its subsequent light as a sign of God's intervention in Jewish history.

Menorahs—or *hanukiot*—are lit for eight days to commemorate that miracle. A menorah is a nine-branched candelabrum: eight candle or oil holders are for the eight nights of the holiday, and the ninth holder is for the *shamash,* the light used to ignite the others.

The menorah can be made from a wide selection of nonflammable materials— glazed ceramics, copper, silver, brass, stone, glass, pewter—and can vary in size and shape. Some artisans set the candle or oil holders in a straight line; others stagger them in height or even place them in a circle.

Sometimes a menorah will highlight the time and place of its origin. To combine his joy at living in freedom in America, Manfred Anson, an immigrant from Germany, designed a brass menorah with miniature Statues of Liberty at each candle holder (part of the Hebrew Union College-Skirball Museum collection in Los Angeles).

Menorahs today have become a fabulous blend of old ritual and new cultural experiences. Israeli David Azulay, of Sephardic origin, fashions his ceramic menorahs with Moorish designs and colors. American artist Sandra Kravitz interprets the ancient Tree of Life theme in a silver menorah.

Menorahs may also be of stark, simple, modernistic lines such as those designed by Rafi Landau, a contemporary Israeli artist, and Ludwig Wolpert, the famous New York silversmith. Other modern menorahs are tall ornate silver hanukiot with large eagles at the top such as were found in Eastern European synagogues in the last century.

Where to Purchase a Menorah?

Menorahs can be bought in Judaica shops found in synagogues and in the community at large. Some department stores carry menorahs distributed by fine pottery firms. If your community offers a Jewish artisans' festival, you will be able to find a selection of menorahs there.

However, if you live in a community far from a large Jewish population, mail order is your answer. One such catalog is *The Source for Everything Jewish: Hamakor Judaica, Inc.,* Mail Order Department, P.O. Box 48836, Niles, Illinois 60648.

Where to Put the Menorah?

The menorah is placed on a windowsill or table facing the street to publicize the two miracles of Hanukkah: the miracle of the vat of oil and the miracle of Jewish survival. However, in dangerous times, one may place the Hanukkah menorah so that it is not visible from the outside. The light from the menorah should not be used to see by; this light is only used for the commemoration of the miracles.

Lighting the Lights

The major ritual for Hanukkah is the lighting of the menorah, which takes place soon after nightfall, or as soon as the household is together. On Friday night, the Hanukkah candles are lit first, followed by the Shabbat candles, as traditionally fire is not created on the Sabbath itself.

Some people prefer an oil-burning menorah. They may feel it is more authentic, while some folks simply like the smell of olive oil burning slowly. Others choose to use candles for ease in use and for their bright, warm colors.

LIGHT THAT MENORAH!

1. *The shamash, or serving candle, is lit first, for it then is used to light the others.*

2. *On the first night of the holiday, the first candle is placed in the far right side of the menorah (as you stand facing it).*

3. *Each candle should reflect the number of nights of the holiday thus far. On each night following the first night, add an additional candle to the left of the previous night's candle. For example, on the second night, add one candle to the left of the first night's candle so two candles* will glow. *On the eighth day, the last candle is placed in the far left cup, and then all eight candles will burn brightly.*

4. *The candles are lit each evening starting from the left side to the right, always lighting the current night's candle first. For example, on the third night of Hanukkah, light candle number three first, then number two, then number one.*

5. *After lighting the other candles, replace the shamash in its holder.*

Why are the candles lit in this precise order? A debate was recorded in the Talmud when two rabbinical schools were asserting their views on the appropriate pattern for lighting the Hanukkah lights. The school of Rabbi Shammai maintained: "On the first day, eight lights are lit and thereafter they are gradually reduced by one each day." But the school of Rabbi Hillel responded saying: "On the first day one is lit and thereafter they are progressively increased." And Hillel went on to explain that we increase and enhance the light, for we increase and enhance holiness in the world (*Talmud Babli,* Shabbat, 21a). The latter opinion prevailed.

In many homes the household members take turns lighting the menorah, giving men, women, and children the privilege of lighting. Some people light several menorahs and enjoy the flames as the many menorahs glow brightly.

Two blessings are sung each night as the candles are lit. The blessings emphasize the theme of the miracle that God performed for Jews long ago. Jews today hope that God continues to create miracles for them as well. The *Shehehayanu* prayer is recited on the first night only.

Each night the celebration continues with songs or readings that highlight the meanings of Hanukkah. Additional songs, games, and gifts are often part of the festivities.

The song "Rock of Ages" is a well-known Hanukkah favorite. A fun Hanukkah tape, which includes "Rock of Ages," "Light One Candle," and some other favorites is *Chanukah with Cindy.* If you cannot find it locally, write to: Cindy Paley, 14246 Chandler Blvd., Van Nuys, CA 91401.

SYNAGOGUE TRADITIONS

Hanukkah is celebrated with the lighting of candles each evening in the synagogue as in the home. Many temples encourage different groups within the synagogue to join for dinner and programs surrounding the menorah lighting.

In all daily services, *Al HaNissim* is added in the *Amidah,* the silent prayer. Al HaNissim highlights the many miracles that God performed for our ancestors and continues for us.

In the morning services the *Hallel* prayer is sung daily and the *Torah* is read. The Torah readings are taken from the book of Numbers, focusing on the story of rededication.

On the Shabbat morning during Hanukkah the *Haftarah* reading from Zechariah 2:14–4:7 is included. This reading was chosen because it contains a motto for Hanukkah: "Not by might, not by power, but by spirit alone shall all people live in peace." Some synagogues may also add dramatic readings from the Book of Maccabees, or even contemporary plays that highlight Hanukkah themes.

INSIGHTS

From Darkness into Light

Hanukkah takes place during the darkest days of the winter season. Like other cultures, Judaism experiences the winter solstice and the darkness, which represents endless time, confusion, and gloom. But in response to the dark of winter, Jews bring light into their lives.

Light adds hope and knowledge to the confusion. Light encourages a forward look, a chance to celebrate that life will be better, that darkness, even despair, can change to a world that enjoys light, a world that has opportunity.

Stand Strong Against the Tide

Although Greek culture was appealing to many Jews, there were a few strong souls who resisted the temptation to acculturate. Those few, those Maccabees, serve as models that we might emulate today.

Standing tall against outside influences can be necessary in family life and in business. The pull of making it big, quickly and easily, maybe even unethically, must be restrained. The ability to be honest in a deceitful world requires Maccabean strength.

Jews Are a Minority in a Majority World

Outside of Israel Jews represent a tiny percentage of their countries' populations. Most Jews choose to live in large urban centers, to feel the support of other Jewish families and to be able to enjoy certain benefits that the large Jewish community experience can provide. However, many Jews live in areas where they are reminded almost daily that they are a minority amidst a majority culture.

As a minority, Jews may sometimes feel that they sit on the fringe of secular life while experiencing different holidays. Significant Jewish times of the year—spring and fall—do not fit into the normal holiday periods. Jews celebrate the Sabbath on Friday night and Saturday, not Sunday. They often speak a Jewish language, depending on their country of origin: Hebrew, Yiddish, Ladino, Farsi. They often eat with a concern for a unique preparation of food—*kashrut*. They have a special alliance with another nation—Israel.

All these cultural dimensions define Jews as one of the minorities within secular society. Celebration and practice of their traditions assist Jews to develop pride in who they are.

Religious Questioning

But for some adults and children, pride is mixed with uncertainty. For sometimes we want to be like others, we want to join in with the dominant life-style, we want to be accepted.

That is the tip of the ambivalence that some Jews may feel in December as Christmas looms large, powerful, and dramatic. We can feel the excitement as we notice the streets decorated with lights, the store windows designed with warm winter scenes of homes with trees and fireplaces. We are reminded that we Jews live in a Christian country, that we do not experience one of the major Christian religious holy days.

At Christmas, Christians celebrate the anniversary of the birth of the Christian messiah, Jesus. The evergreen tree stands as a religious symbol of the everlasting, ever-present faith in Jesus as their messiah. Some early Christian legends assert that on the night Jesus was born all the trees of the forest bloomed and bore fruit despite the winter snow and ice. The tree is still meant today to symbolize the resurrection and immortality of Jesus.

Santa Claus originated as Saint Nicholas, a fourth-century bishop of Myra, Turkey. He became the patron saint of travelers and sailors when on a pilgrimage to the Holy Land. He later became a patron saint for children because legend attributes a miracle to him: He saved three homeless boys who had been brutally beaten by a shopkeeper.

Mistletoe and the green Christmas wreath represent the crown of thorns placed on the head of Jesus by Roman soldiers. The little berries represent the drops of his blood.

All these symbols carry immense power because the Christian religious community incorporates them as symbols that are invested with religious meaning. Although Easter is the religious central holiday in the Christian holiday cycle, Christmas is certainly the most culturally popular holiday; it is definitely the major winter festival in the secular calendar.

Sometimes it may be uncomfortable for Jews because we do not mirror the majority holiday. But that reality in and of itself is the message of Hanukkah. We do not have to join the majority. Rather, we assert our freedom to enjoy our own values, customs, and traditions. We respect our own faith, and then we can respect and enjoy others'. We assert the right to be different and to be proud of our differences. We can communicate these realities to our children at all ages and stages.

THERE IS NO SANTA CLAUS

I grew up in a small midwestern town with very few Jews. So I suspect it was with some trepidation that my mother told my younger brother and me at an early age that there was no Santa Claus. She explained that while this was true, we were not to tell the other children and ruin their holiday for them. And we didn't tell.

Each year I would be called upon to bring a menorah to school and tell the story of Hanukkah to my entire class, and to explain why I didn't celebrate Christmas. When we had to sing Christmas carols in school assemblies, I would mouth the words, conscious that these were not my songs, my holiday.

Although our house was practically the only house without Christmas decorations and a tree, I never felt that I wanted to participate in Christmas. My parents were able to instill the belief that Christmas was the Christians' holiday and we Jews had our own holidays of which to be proud. And to this day I am grateful for this strong sense of Jewish identity that I learned at a young age.

—P.Z.M.

Hanukkah and Christmas are celebrated around the same time. Other than the fact that they both add light to the winter darkness, there are no similarities. At Hanukkah we Jews bring out our menorahs, our dreidels, our frying pans for latkes. There is no such symbol as a Hanukkah bush or stocking, although certain commercial elements would encourage us to take on these Christian customs.

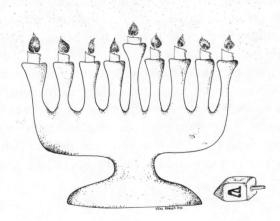

Perhaps Hanukkah has been given a popularity boost because of its proximity to Christmas. Hanukkah, Yom Kippur, and Pesach are the most widely observed Jewish holidays in the United States, but Hanukkah remains the minor holiday of the three within the Jewish holiday cycle.

HOW DO YOU SPELL THAT HOLIDAY?

You might think that "Hanukkah" is the only way to spell this holiday week. However, look at these variations:

Chanukah
Channukah
Chanukkah

Hanuka
Hanukah
and so on . . .
Hebrew sounds written in English letters will keep us guessing. Is this a game or what?

ACTIVITIES

Because Hanukkah is celebrated for eight nights and the ritual requirements are simple, the holiday can be enhanced by assigning unique themes and activities to different nights. Here are various possibilities:

1. Big neighborhood party: Decorate, do holiday food "made with oil" (if you are rushed, don't forget frozen latkes—fried potato pancakes eaten with applesauce or sour cream—and ready-made *sufganiot*—jelly donuts), emphasize the celebration through song, stories, skits, and games.

2. Game night: Play dreidel—the four-sided top whose sides are marked by four letters of the Hebrew alphabet that stand for: "A Great Miracle Happened Here." Gather together nuts or toothpicks or pennies and divide the ante among two to six players. Each person places one ante in the center of the circle. Take turns spinning the dreidel. If it falls on:

a. the Hebrew letter *nun,* the player gets nothing;

b. the Hebrew letter *gimmel,* the player takes all from the center pot, and now all the players must replenish the center pot with one ante each;

c. the Hebrew letter *hay,* the player gets half the center pot;

d. the Hebrew letter *shin,* the player puts in one ante from his/her stash.
The winner is the one who has the most at the end of the game (end at any time that you want).

3. Art projects can be fun for the holiday:

a. Dreidels can be purchased or made. A basic dreidel can be made in this way: Make a 1-inch cube from construction paper. Write one of the four Hebrew letters for the dreidel (see above) on each side of the cube. Use a colorful felt tip pen. Pierce the center of the cube with a short pencil and spin.

One can also make a dreidel from clay. Shape clay into a 1-inch cube. Add a small pyramid shape to the bottom of the cube and a $1'' \times \frac{1}{4}''$ stem to the top. Let dry for two days, then paint with tempura colors. Paint the four Hebrew letters, one on each side. Allow two days to dry. Paint with white glue to hold the colors. Let dry two days, and play dreidel.

b. Menorahs can also be made at home. Get one strip of wood about 12″ long and 2″ deep × 2″ wide. Go to hardware store and buy nine ½-inch nuts. Mark 9 places on the wood strip, about 1¼ inches apart. Glue each nut to the wood. These nuts serve as candle holders for the menorah. You can use upside-down bottle caps as well. Either paint the menorah with tempura paints or spray with gold or silver glitter spray paint. Let dry and use for Hanukkah.

Clay is also a good material for menorah making. Roll clay into a long, snakelike shape. Curve one side of the menorah for the shamash, the candle that will light the others. Pierce the clay with a pencil to create candle holders. Let dry completely. After two days, paint with tempura or spray paints. Enjoy!

These can be used to decorate your home or given as gifts. Before they are used, make sure the menorahs are not flammable.

4. Reading nights: Short stories by Isaac Bashevis Singer in the collection *The Power of Light: Eight Stories for Hanukkah* (New York: Avon Books, 1982) could be read one per night. *Eight Tales for Eight Nights* written by storytellers Penina Schram and Steven M. Rosman (Northvale, New Jersey: Jason Aronson, Inc., 1990) is a great collection of Jewish stories from all over the globe with musical notations for Hanukkah songs.

Another fun book is *The Animated Menorah: Travels on a Space Dreidel* by Ephraim Sidon (London: Scopus Films, 1986). Read a chapter each night and enjoy the claymation illustrations by Rony Oren.

5. Sports: Any athletes in your neighborhood? Create your own Israeli torch relay as it is run annually from Modin, battleground of the Maccabees, to Jerusalem! In your neighborhood, your relay can start as you light a menorah and begin the evening celebration.

6. Hanukkah photo night: Document the Hanukkah celebrations at your home: give each household member an empty photo album, have each person gather pictures, and make albums. Add new photos each year and document your family history.

7. Have family members each write a letter to a non-Jewish friend explaining the history and importance of Hanukkah. Share your letters with each other and mail!

8. Make a *tzedakah* night, for "charity begins at home." On one night of Hanukkah, collect the money that might have been used for gifts and decide as a family: Where can we make a difference? What individual or agency could benefit from this gift? Prepare for the night by asking children and adults to learn about their favorite projects and present their information to the family. Vote to decide where you will contribute.

9. Invite a new immigrant family or senior citizens to your home for Hanukkah. Ask them to share their memories and traditions with your family. Share your country's Jewish customs.

10. On one night of Hanukkah, try to go to a concert or play with another family to celebrate the holiday. You can light candles, sing, have a simple dinner, and then enjoy a little culture together.

11. Collect a piece of Jewish art: Menorah or dreidel collecting can add precious heirlooms.

12. Cooking night: Make latkes or *kugel* from scratch (how many pounds of potatoes?—see Senta's recipe on page 100) or make sugar cookies and cut out in Hanukkah shapes.

13. Decorations can be made or purchased. Use your creativity and have fun! Make banners from construction paper—cut out menorah and dreidel shapes and paste them onto the banner. Or cut out six-pointed Jewish stars from color felt and string them together with felt dreidel shapes. Hang up in your living room and enjoy the homemade spirit of Hanukkah.

14. So let's talk about gifts. Hanukkah is a celebration with so many activities that we can hardly include them all, yet children and adults in the United States also associate Hanukkah with gift giving. In previous generations, children received Hanukkah *gelt*, money, from all the relatives. Now some families choose to give gifts on some but not all the evenings. Sometimes the gifts are special and sometimes they are the basics (oh, yes, pajamas, slippers, and new socks . . . Ah, Mom!). Try to balance gifts with activities and tzedakah giving.

RECIPES

Hanukkah is one of those holidays that offers opportunities for those of us who are still partial to fried foods. The theme of this holiday: Bathe it in oil. For simplicity and time saving, consider some of the frozen latkes now available. They will do in a pinch, although the recipe included here is superior!

SENTA'S LATKES—GERMAN-STYLE POTATO PANCAKES

1 small whole onion, finely chopped
2 cups raw, peeled, grated white potatoes
1 whole egg (or for a light version, two egg whites)
1 tsp. salt
1 tsp. pepper
1 Tbsp. flour (can add a bit more if batter is too thin)
olive oil as needed

Wash and peel the potatoes. Grate them coarsely. Mix with chopped onion. Drain as much of the water/juice off the mixture as possible. Add eggs and other ingredients. Mix.

Heat enough olive oil to completely cover the skillet. Drop mixture by large spoonfuls to make 2–3-inch-diameter patties. Brown; turn and brown other side. Serve with sour cream, cottage cheese, or applesauce.

POTATO KUGEL

6 Tbsp. olive oil
1 onion, chopped fine
7 raw potatoes, grated and drained
3 well-beaten eggs (or 6 egg whites)
½ cup flour
½ tsp. baking powder
2 tsp. salt
½ tsp. pepper

Heat 2 tablespoons of olive oil in skillet and cook the onion. Place potatoes, beaten eggs, flour, baking powder, oil, salt, and pepper into bowl and mix well. Add the cooked onions. Stir. Grease a 9″ × 13″ baking pan and pour mixture in. Bake at 400 degrees for one hour. Serve immediately or freeze and reheat prior to serving.

HANUKKAH BLESSINGS

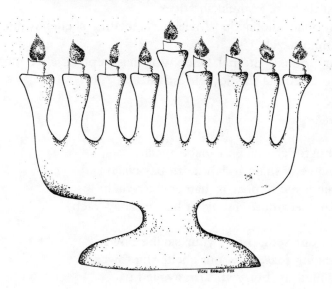

Introductory meditation to be recited together before candle lighting:

Today we thank God for all the goodness in our lives, for the beauty of nature, for the love we feel for one another, for the Hanukkah tradition.
May our celebration increase the light of freedom in the world.

Candle lighting:
(Put the candles into the menorah from right to left; however, light them from left to right. On the Shabbat of Hanukkah, light the Hanukkah lights first, then those for Shabbat.)

Baruch Ata Adonai Elohaynu Melech Haolam, asher keedshanu b'meetzvotav v'tzeevanu l'hadleek ner shel Hanukkah.
Blessed are You Adonai, Eternal One, Who enables us to welcome Hanukkah by kindling these lights.

Baruch Ata Adonai Elohaynu Melech Haolam, She'ahsah Neeseem l'avotaynu baya-meem hahem, baz'man hazeh.
Blessed are You Adonai, Eternal One, Who made miracles for our ancestors, in times and seasons past.

Shehehayanu:

(On the first night of Hanukkah add:)

Baruch Ata Adonai Elohaynu Melech Haolam, shehehayanu, v'keeyomanu v'higeeyanu laz'man hazeh.

Blessed are You Adonai, Eternal One, Who has kept us alive, sustained us, and encouraged us to celebrate this joyful festival.

(Continue singing:)

Rock of Ages:

Ma-oz tsur Yeshuati l'cha na'eh l'shabe'ayach;

Tikon bayt t'feelatee, v'sham todah ne'za bayayach.

L'ayt tacheen matbayach, meetzar hamenabay-yach.

Az egmor b'sheer meezmor, Hanukkat ha meezbay-yach.

Rock of Ages, let our song praise your saving power.

You, amid the raging foes, were our sheltering tower.

Furious they assailed us, but your arm availed us,

And your word broke their sword

When our own strength failed us.

7

TU B'SHVAT—THE JEWISH
ECOLOGY DAY

AN agricultural holiday that looks forward to the spring season, Tu B'Shvat is the celebration of the earth and its produce. Tu B'Shvat is a Hebrew abbreviation linking two Hebrew letters, *tet* and *vav*, which numerically total fifteen. The name means the 15th day of the winter month of *Shvat*, which usually occurs in January.

In ancient times, Tu B'Shvat was also a tax day, marking the day after which all fruit harvested would be included in the next year's calculations for the tithe, the percent of the harvest that Jewish farmers brought to the Temple in Jerusalem as a contribution.

Tu B'Shvat is based on themes found throughout the Bible and specifically in Genesis, in which humans and God share partnership in concern for the natural environment. Humans take responsibility to care for the earth and God cares for the whole of the universe.

A Talmudic story associated with Tu B'Shvat describes this concern:

Roman Emperor: What are you doing, Old Man?

Honi, the Old Man: I am planting a carob tree.

Roman Emperor: How long will it take before the tree bears fruit?

Honi: About ten years.

Roman Emperor: Surely you do not expect to live that long. You won't be able to enjoy your own tree!

Honi: When I came here, I found trees planted by those who lived before me. I simply am planting as they did, so that those who come after me will enjoy the fruit of my labor.

HOME TRADITIONS

Although Tu B'Shvat begins in the evening, as do all Jewish holidays, no candles are lit as this is a holiday in which there are no restrictions placed on work; it is not a day of rest. There is no particular greeting for the holiday, although *"Hag Sameach—Happy Holiday"* is always appropriate.

Jews celebrate this holiday by eating the seven types of plant produce that are cited in Deuteronomy 8:8: wheat, barley, grapes, figs, pomegranates, olives, and date honey. Today people often add contemporary fruits: oranges, avocados, bananas, and kiwi. Carob, known as *bokser* in Yiddish and as St. John's Bread, is also eaten on Tu B'Shvat.

Based on sixteenth-century mystical traditions, some people celebrate Tu B'Shvat with a *seder,* a home service for the evening or daytime that has a specific order. Themes of the seder might include: reclamation of the land of Israel, concern for the earth as a total environment, planting for the future, links between trees and the *Torah*—the Tree of Life—and the human role as caretaker of the earth.

The Tu B'Shevat seder is not a fixed ritual. It might be structured like the

Passover seder: with four cups of wine, special fruits as symbols, different sections emphasizing the various themes. Creative potential abounds to enhance this seder with contemporary stories, poetry, and art.

EVERY BLADE OF GRASS HAS AN ANGEL ATTACHED TO IT

Rabbi Simeon bar Yochai said: Three things are equal in importance: earth, humans, and rain. Rabbi Levi ben Hayyata said: And these three words each consist of three letters in Hebrew. Why? To teach that without earth there would be no rain and without rain there would be no earth. Without either, human beings could not exist.

Midrash, Genesis Rabbah 13.3

SYNAGOGUE TRADITIONS

On Tu B'Shvat, Jews participate in a regular daily service, although synagogues may link readings to biblical texts, such as Genesis 1:11–13, Leviticus 19:23–25, or Psalm 65:10–12. These texts highlight the human relationship to the earth and our responsibility to care for the earth. In addition, temples may emphasize Jewish concern for the land of Israel and encourage people to purchase trees to be planted in Israel.

Some temples celebrate a Tu B'Shvat seder and encourage tree planting and recycling on synagogue grounds.

INSIGHTS

The Human Caretaker

At the time that God created the very first human being, God took him and had him inspect the trees in the Garden of Eden. God said to the first human: Look at how lovely and outstanding all my work has turned out to be. Please note that everything I've created I created for you. Think about this carefully and do not damage or destroy my world. For if you do . . . there is no one to repair it (Ecclesiastes Rabba 7:28).

Each human being has the ongoing responsibility to care for the earth. The link emphasized in this text serves to remind each adult and each child that human action counts. If human actions lead to destruction, there is no second chance.

Therefore, by celebrating this holiday, Jews remember and remind others that their concern for the land and its produce is not a trend but a lifetime commitment.

Torah as the Tree of Life

The imagery of trees for Jews is quite important: The Torah itself is often referred to as the Tree of Life. As a tree nurtures, protects, and provides sustenance for those living around it, so the Torah guides, protects, and provides spiritual sustenance. Even the wooden poles used to scroll the entire Torah parchment are called *atzeem,* the Hebrew word for trees.

ACTIVITIES

1. It is a tradition to plant trees in Israel for this holiday, and you, too, can plant a tree—or a forest! Call or write to Jewish National Fund, 42 E. 69th Street, New York, NY 10021, (212) 879-9300 or (800) 542-8733.

In ancient times parents planted a tree when a new baby was born. Today, this custom is reappearing as new parents purchase trees. And if you do so in honor or in memory of someone, JNF will acknowledge this gift to the recipient or the recipient's family.

JNF was established in the 1920s to purchase and develop land in Israel for Jewish settlements. This international organization plays a key role in developing Israeli farming techniques such as irrigation and plant rotation.

2. Explore your home: What products are from trees? Tally your list. Consider the importance of trees for life, for protection, for reflection.

3. Family trees—Tu B'Shvat is another opportunity to draw up the family tree (see the chapter on Sukkot for ideas on this project) and talk about the work our ancestors did to ensure a world for us. What will we do for our children?

4. Make a *Tu B'Shvat* seder at home.

5. Read *The Butter Battle Book* by Dr. Seuss (New York: Random House, 1984). This poignant story describes the horrors of wars on earth. Share your thoughts regarding our role in keeping the world a safe place to live. Discuss fears and hopes. In addition, you all may enjoy reading *The Giving Tree* by Shel Silverstein (New York: Harper and Row, 1964).

6. If you haven't already started, prepare your home for recycling: Separate cans, glass, plastic, paper. Find the nearest recycling center, and as a family get involved in saving the earth.

7. Learn to shop with the earth in mind. Use cloth shopping bags, buy recycled paper and products for your home and office. Each of us has the opportunity to make a difference in our world. Recycle clothes through the Salvation Army or your local National Council of Jewish Women or other social service agency.

8. Plant your own herbs and spices, even if you only have a windowsill. Encourage children to experience caring for a plant, watching it grow, harvesting, and eating the crop. Plant parsley and basil now, use it for your Passover seder later.

9. Visit a tree nursery and learn to identify different trees and the length of time various trees need to grow to maturity. Identify native Israeli plants and vegetables.

10. Join *Shomrei Adamah,* the Keepers of the Earth, a Jewish environmental group. Write to: *Shomrei Adamah,* Church Road and Greenwood Avenue, Wnycote, PA 19095.

RECIPES

FRUIT COMPOTE

½ cup dried apricots

½ cup dried nectarines

½ cup raisins

2–3 chopped and peeled apples

1 cup sweet red wine

½ tsp. cinnamon

½ tsp. cloves

Add all ingredients and cook slowly for several hours. Add water if needed. Let cool to room temperature and enjoy.

Serves approximately 6.

8
PURIM—THE JEWISH MARDI GRAS

O once there was a wicked wicked man
    And Haman was his name, Sir.
  He tried to murder all the Jews,
Though they were not to blame, Sir.
    O today we'll merry merry be
    O today we'll merry merry be
    And nosh some hamentaschen.

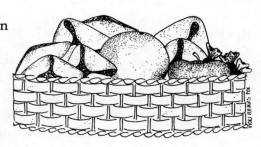

PURIM is a fun-filled Jewish holiday that takes place on the 14th of the Hebrew month of *Adar* in the early spring (February or March). Jews celebrate with silliness and abandon. It is a time to dress up, to repeat silly rhymes, to hear the *Megillah*—the story of Purim—and to party.

Purim is based on the events found in the biblical Book of Esther. Esther was a Jew who risked her life to stand up against Haman, the closest advisor of the Persian King Ahashuerus. Encouraged by her uncle Mordechai, Esther convinced the king to turn against Haman.

The name of Purim is understood to be derived from the word *"pur,"* which means "to draw lots." In the biblical story, the evil Haman drew lots for the date and time that the Jews were to be annihilated. However, when Haman died *on that very day,* the day was transformed from "one of grief and mourning, to one of pure joy" (Esther 9:22) for the entire Jewish people.

The story of Purim depicts how Jews have lived in a non-Jewish environment and survived against a powerful government. One might ask: Is the story of Purim factual? Time, dates, places, and names may or may not be. The events cited in the Book of Esther are understood to have taken place in Persia around the fifth century B.C.E.

However, the Purim message—that Jews can overcome a hateful enemy against tremendous odds—is as important in our day as when the holiday of Purim was first celebrated. Jews have struggled with Haman and Hitler and other fanatics, yet the Jewish people still survive.

GREETINGS

"Hag Sameach—Happy Holiday" is the greeting for Purim.

HOME TRADITIONS

Preparations

The home customs of Purim come from the Book of Esther:

> And Mordechai wrote these things and sent letters unto all the Jews that were in all the provinces of the King Ahashuerus to remind them to keep the fourteenth of Adar, and the fifteenth the same, the days in which Jews had rested from their enemies and the month which was turned from sorrow to joy, from mourning into a good day. Then they should make days of feasting and gladness, of sending portions one to another and gifts to the poor (Esther 9:20–22).

One of the special customs of Purim is the giving of *Mishloach Manot,* simple gifts. When preparing these treats to give to friends and relatives, it is fun to make baked goods or homemade crafts that are easy to prepare and deliver. (See "Activities.")

Equally important as giving to friends and family is giving to the poor. This is known as *Matanot L'evyonim,* gifts for the needy. It's especially thoughtful to give gifts in person. Instead of simply sending a check to an agency, also visit a home for the aged, volunteer at a food pantry, or spend a day helping new immigrants.

A "GOODIE" ALTERNATIVE

This year for Purim, due to the economic realities of the country, instead of spending money on baskets of Purim treats, I decided to give an equivalent donation to Mazon—the national Jewish organization to feed the hungry (2940 Westwood Blvd., Suite 7, Los Angeles, CA 90064). As my children enjoy personally delivering mishloach manot *to our friends and neighbors, I came up with the following plan:*

From a local candy store I bought several chocolate bars (about 2 inches × 4 inches in diameter) with the words "Happy Purim" and a gragger and mask molded on them. The store wrapped the bars (one for each household) in clear plastic and tied a little blue ribbon around the bars.

Then the children made a card with the aid of a computer program. The cover, decorated with champagne and a piece of cake (the program doesn't have hamentaschen designs), said: "What's Purim Without Goodies?" The inside explained that we were giving a contribution to Mazon this year in honor of the recipients. (We included Mazon's address in case anyone else also wanted to contribute.)

We made copies of the card, folded each one, and punched a hole in the top left-hand corner. We then tied the card to the wrapped candy bar by pulling the ends of the ribbon through the punched hole.

The result was a beautiful miniature gift that the children could still deliver and which received tremendously favorable comments. (This also provided a mathematics lesson as we calculated how much money to donate in honor of each household and the total contribution.) So wasn't this a "goodie" alternative?

—P.Z.M.

Purim is in effect the Jewish Mardi Gras. It gives children and adults a safe and sanctioned occasion to dress up. Many children and adults spend weeks planning their coming year's Purim costumes. Sometimes folks appear as the lead characters in the Esther story; others dress as contemporary political and social figures. People wear costumes to the temple Megillah reading and to Purim parties. Do up your face, put on a hat, and have a blast!

Evening

As the celebration begins with the onset of the evening, a simple dinner is served at home. However, no candles are lit. Why? Purim is a holiday with no restrictions on work; it is not a day of rest. After dinner, the celebration continues with the Megillah reading at temple.

Daytime

During the late afternoon of the day of Purim, several hours after the morning service, families may gather for a *Seudat Purim,* a festive meal. This can be a time for Purim skits, songs, and imaginative children's plays. Enjoy the lightness and ease of this celebration in your home.

SYNAGOGUE TRADITIONS

Shabbat Prior to Purim

The Shabbat prior to Purim is known as Shabbat Zachor, in which the Torah portion recalling the actual exodus is read. After the Jewish people escaped from Egypt they were attacked by surprise. The warrior Amalek and his nation tried to destroy the Jews at their most vulnerable moment—physically weak and demoralized after the years of slavery in Egypt.

The biblical text cites an important command: "Therefore, when the Lord your God grants you safety from all your enemies, you shall blot out the memory of Amalek from under heaven. Do not forget!" (See Deuteronomy 25:17–19, Exodus 17: 8–16.)

Amalek was intent on destroying the Jewish people. In addition, Amalek encouraged others to destroy the Jews as well. The Jewish tradition responded: Blot out Amalek! Wipe out and forget the eternal enemy of the Jews, and yet, in reality, Jews cannot forget.

Haman, the evil scoundrel in the Book of Esther, was believed to be a descendant of Amalek. Both Haman and Amalek were intent on destroying the Jews. Yet the Jewish people survived those tyrants and many more.

So on Purim at temple when the Megillah is read, Jews continue the tradition of blotting out Amalek—they stamp and scream each time the name of Haman is pronounced.

The Megillah

The holiday's pivotal ritual is the reading of the Megillah, the Book of Esther. It is read twice: once during the evening service and once the following morning.

The Megillah is a handwritten scroll, similar in style to the Torah, except that, in contrast to the Torah, the Megillah can be an illuminated manuscript.

SO WHAT'S THE BIG DEAL?

A Yiddish phrase you may have heard is "A ganze megillah!" The ganze megillah is a long, involved story, and could be used to refer to a long, highfalutin story that is as curious as the Purim tale itself. Keep this phrase in mind and use it accordingly.

The Megillah text is chanted to musical notes unique to the holiday. It is usually sung by a cantor, congregant, or Hebrew school student. Many synagogues ensure that people understand this important book by also reading it out loud in English.

If you come to a synagogue for the first time during Purim, you might think all order has been abandoned by the Jewish people. Every time the name of Haman is read, people boo and hiss, scream and bang. *Graggers*—noisemakers—are used to blot out the memory. In the past in some European cities, the name of Haman was written on stones and every time the name was mentioned the stones were banged together.

In some congregations, when Esther is mentioned the congregants applaud or shout "Hurray!" Some bring flowers and throw them when Esther is named.

Children and adults are in costumes, and frequently wine and other libations are in evidence. Look out for careening clowns, scary monsters, futuristic space creatures, rough-and-tough cowhands, and your "favorite" political figures.

Many synagogues celebrate Purim with large carnivals a few days before or after Purim. This adds to the Mardi Gras–like atmosphere of the holiday and is frequently used to benefit the synagogue as a fund-raising event.

INSIGHTS

No God in the Text

It is curious that although the Book of Esther is biblical, nowhere in it is God's name mentioned. The Book of Esther is a tale of a woman cleverly saving her people.

Purim stresses the message that human beings must work for their own survival. God does not pull the strings from on high to change the social and political circumstances, but God will quietly imbue people with strength to survive against unbelievable odds.

Despite conditions where the greater numbers seem to overpower the few, Jews learn not to despair but to act. It is human action that is validated.

On Addictions

Purim is a "strange" holiday, one in which the world is turned upside down. Determination overcomes power, weakness overcomes military strength, the few overturn the many.

Historically, Jews have been bound by rules that govern behaviors of every waking moment. The Purim command to drink oneself into oblivion so that we cannot recognize the difference between "cursed be Haman" and "blessed be Mordechai," was a topsy-turvy custom that emphasized the topsy-turvy nature of Purim.

This drinking was in direct contrast to expected behaviors for Jews regarding the consumption of alcohol. Alcohol is provided for in Jewish custom—albeit in moderation—as one way by which holidays and Shabbat are welcomed.

In the past, when alcohol addiction was not as recognized a problem in all segments of society as it is now, Jews could easily participate in this one-day drunken abandon. Today Jews struggle with alcoholism as do other peoples.

Judaism should reconsider the emphasis on drinking at Purim in light of the possible consequences of this behavior. By changing this focus, we can encourage individuals to overcome self-destructive behaviors.

Today we can blot out the names of Amalek, Haman, and Hitler by talking about the terrors and learning to cope with the pain rather than obliterating ourselves in denial. This dialogue recognizes the distrust and disappointment that exists between different people and can bridge those gaps. Continued dialogue between Jews and other nations and religions is a healthy way to cope with anti-Semitism.

ACTIVITIES

1. It is fun to participate in the custom of Mishloach Manot, the giving of gifts to family and friends on Purim. If you have the time and inclination, bake *hamentaschen* (the special three-cornered Purim pastry usually filled with prune, jelly, or poppy seeds) or make crafts projects. For those with limited free time, gifts of simple purchased items delivered in a basket or a notice that a contribution has been given in someone's honor are equally good ways to participate in this tradition.

Many folks enjoy decorating the boxes and bags in which the gifts are sent. Some people fill colored paper plates with goodies and then staple the ends of the plates to look like hamentaschen. Others use fancy "lunch bags" and staple the top of the bag to come to a point as if it were the top corner of the hamentaschen. Still others fill elaborate wicker baskets with all types of breads, pastries, and liquor.

2. Parents and children together can decide what *Matanot L'evyonim*—gifts for the poor—will be given to whom. This is a valuable lesson in determining what is a gift, what we give, and how we feel when we give to others in need.

3. The Book of Esther highlights a Jewish female leader. Parents and children together might research the ways that the following women and others have contributed uniquely to Jewish life and survival: the biblical leaders Rebeccah, Yael, and Deborah; the historical personages Bruriah and Gluckel; and the modern heroes Golda Meir, Bella Abzug, Sally Priesand, Sally Ride, and Barbra Streisand.

4. Write a modern Purim story. Include poetry, music, humor, and rap in your delivery. Present it to family and friends on Purim. Your skit might be a radio broadcast, interview, spoof of current government officials. Be wild and have fun!

5. Younger children will enjoy making puppets to illustrate the Purim story. Use paper bags or socks. Decorate with felt, pipe cleaners, buttons, yarn, and feathers. Bring your puppet to the Megillah reading.

6. Much of Purim is theater. Go to a play as a family. Discover how a play is developed from a story line, story to scene development, development to delivery. Explore the power of the life on stage and link that experience to the drama of the Purim story.

7. Get into the arts. Make graggers that can be used to blot out Haman's name. Masks can add to your costume; use papier-mâché, foil, or cardboard.

MAKE THAT MASK!

So someone wants to be Esther or even Haman? A simple papier-mâché mask can be started a week ahead of time:

1. Use a ball or balloon as a base as you shape foil paper over it into the image of a face with eyes, nose, hair, etc. Keep it simple.

2. Make a liquidy paste out of flour and water. Dip strips of newspaper into the paste. Drain the strips and place them on the foil. Cover all sections, leaving holes for the eyes and mouth. Let the mask dry for a day.

3. After it is dry, use poster paints to paint the face with all its details. Again, let it sit for a day.

4. Paint white glue on the inside of the mask to secure its shape and let it dry. The following day, to protect the mask, paint white glue over the face of the mask. Paint only one direction, as the underlying paint may smear.

5. With a cape or jacket you, my dear, are off to a great Purim!

8. Illustrate your own Megillah scroll using modern or historical art forms: woodcuts, silkscreen printing, calligraphy, line drawing.

9. Visit collections of Megillah scrolls and note the variety in their illustrations. The art forms reflect the time and place of origin, the cultural influences, the types of available materials. What does this tell us about Jews in those times and places?

10. Purim provides an opportunity to begin discussion of anti-Semitism with children. Being prepared for the realities of life in the world can be a powerful shield against unexpected hurt. In this process, parents can raise awareness of the need to develop inner Jewish strength and pride.

For discussion ideas, look to the relationship between Mordechai and Esther: Why does Esther initially hide her Jewish identity? How does her uncle Mordechai encourage her development of Jewish pride? When do we experience similar feelings? How can we express our hopes and fears about being Jewish? Would you consider Esther a significant Jewish hero?

11. For another source of discussion topics, read together the young adult book *The Night Journey* by Kathryn Lasky (New York: Puffin Books, 1986). In this story, thirteen-year-old Rachel's great-grandmother tells how as a nine-year-old she came up with the plan to help her whole family escape from the Russia of the czar, a more modern-day Haman. The story includes reversible Purim costumes (for disguises) and gold coins (for border guard bribes) baked into hamentaschen.

RECIPES

HAMENTASCHEN (HAMAN'S EAR OR POCKET)

DOUGH:
½ lb. margarine, at room temperature
8 tsp. sugar
3¼ cups sifted flour
2 tsp. baking powder
¼ tsp. salt
3 tsp. orange juice

2 eggs (or 4 egg whites)
2 tsp. vanilla

FILLING:
1 jar prune or poppyseed filling
¼ cup chopped nuts
sugar and cinnamon

Cream the margarine and sugar. Sift the dry ingredients and add to margarine and sugar mixture. Mix well. Add the eggs, orange juice, and vanilla. Knead until dough is formed and divide it into 6 sections. Refrigerate until chilled.

Roll out a section of dough onto a floured board. Use a glass as a cutter for forming circles for the hamentaschen shapes. Put a teaspoon of filling into each circle and fold into a triangle by pinching the edges together. Repeat for remaining five sections of dough. Bake in 325-degree oven for 25 minutes.

9
PESACH—
THE FREEDOM STORY

ASK any Jewish child what the eight-day holiday of *Pesach*—Passover—is about and that child is likely to answer: "It's when we eat *matzah* because when the Jews fled from Egypt they didn't have time to wait for their bread to rise."

And while this answer is correct, it does not emphasize the pivotal theme of Pesach: the Jewish people's liberation from Egyptian slavery, an event which changed the Jewish people forever.

In each generation, Jews experience and reexperience that momentous liberation with the annual celebration of the Passover holiday. As we participate in the *seder*—the home service—each person acknowledges that she/he personally moved from slavery to freedom.

Passover occurs in the spring in March or April. It is celebrated for eight days in most communities, although in Reform synagogues and in Israel people celebrate for seven. The first two and last two of the eight days are those in which we focus on family and rest, not work and school. Seder is celebrated on the first two nights.

GREETINGS

"Hag Sameach—Happy Holiday" is the greeting for the Passover holiday.

HOME TRADITIONS

Jews observe Passover by telling the story of the Exodus from Egypt in whichever ways it can best be understood—in the local language, with music, art, drama; eating matzah, the historic unleavened bread that Jews ate while wandering in the desert after the Exodus; and by avoiding *hametz,* a fermented mixture of any one of five types of grains used in basic food products.

Preparation for Passover

Each person prepares for Passover differently in light of one's choices regarding Jewish observances. Preparation for Passover may include a full spring cleaning in the house, with special concentration on the kitchen, removing all hametz from the house, and bringing out dishes and utensils only used for Passover.

Others may simply put aside those products which contain hametz and get ready to celebrate the holiday. No matter what your choices are, the essence is to mark the significance of this holiday.

PASSOVER IN THE U.S. ARMY

During Passover of 1971 my husband was stationed with the U.S. Army in Munich. We'd been married a little over a year and this was the first time we would be making our own seders. Needless to say, it was a little daunting to prepare for Passover far from home in a country we perceived as hostile.

But we had assistance. First, the Jewish Welfare Board sent "kosher for Passover" canned matzah ball soup, matzah, and other Passover food to armed forces personnel throughout the world. We had the basics.

Then the Jewish army chaplain in Munich instructed us on many points. For the first time we cleaned our kitchen to remove all hametz,

even though at that time we didn't have dishes just for Passover. As we cleaned, there was a tremendous feeling of Jewish pride as we continued the ancient Passover ritual in post-Holocaust Germany!

And even today, in support for our women and men serving abroad, we can send contributions (a solo seder kit costs $12) to the JWB Jewish Chaplains Council (formerly known as the Jewish Welfare Board) at: Women's Organizations Services, c/o JWB Associates, 15 East 26th Street, New York, NY 10010-1579. Indicate this is for Passover food and try to send it by February.

—P.Z.M.

What Is Hametz?

Although hametz is technically the fermented mixture of various grains, it symbolically represents the remnants of the bitter Egyptian slave experience. Jews rid themselves of hametz to reexperience freedom from Egyptian bondage, and that is why hametz, the symbol of oppression, is forbidden on Passover.

The foods not permitted on Passover include any mixture of flour and water that is allowed to rise—in other words, what we call breads. Hametz can be made from wheat, barley, rye, oats, spelt. People from European (Ashkenazic) traditions also omit rice, millet, corn, and most beans. Foods such as breads, crackers, cereals, muffins, cakes, and all liquids (including hard liquor) made from those same ingredients are not permissible Passover foods.

For Passover, Jews buy products labeled "kosher for Passover": matzah, matzah balls and mixes, cakes, processed foods, vinegars, wines, and frozen foods. In addition, there are several products that can be purchased as always, provided they are bought new for the holiday: fresh fruits and permissible vegetables, coffee, sugar, tea, salt, pepper, milk, eggs, fish, and meat.

If you have specific questions about anything relating to food for Passover, call up a local synagogue and get some personal advice. Slightly different guidelines for Passover observance exist: An updated kosher directory for Passover is distributed yearly by The Union of Orthodox Jewish Congregations. Write for one at 45 West 36th Street, New York, New York 10017. The Conservative movement adheres to guidelines published by Isaac Klein in *A Guide to Jewish Religious Practice* (New York: Jewish Theological Seminary of America, 1979). The Reform movement follows practices outlined in *Gates of the Seasons,* edited by Peter S. Knobel (New York: Central Conference of American Rabbis, 1983).

Preparation for Seders

Because Passover in its entirety can appear overwhelming, we recommend breaking the whole into manageable parts. As such it becomes a project with specific tasks to be completed by specific times. Use lists to keep the plans and details in order for this year and next. (Even now, after we figure we have a combined experience of having organized over fifty seders, lists help.)

To begin planning, you might consider these questions: Are you having seder at home or are you going as a group to the temple seders? Are you inviting or are you being invited?

Consider inviting those new neighbors, immigrants, or single adults that your local temple may know would appreciate a personal invitation to seder.

If seder is happening at your home, your lists might include notes on these questions: Do you have enough space in the rooms available for the crowd, or can you improvise to use the living room for the seder? Do you need extra tables and chairs (consider renting from a business that delivers, sets up, and picks up)? Can you plan a seating chart that will facilitate a friendly feeling when new and old friends gather for the first time? Can you hire help to serve and clean up so that you can be "free" at the seder?

You may set your table a day ahead of time. It can be a group activity in which all members of the household may participate. Set the plates, silverware, napkins, wine and water glasses, small bowls for salt water (either at individual places or several communal bowls), and individual smaller plates on which to eat the ritual foods.

BALANCING FAMILY SEDERS

An old joke goes, "Why are there two seders?" Answer: "One to go to his family and one to go to hers." And while, of course, this isn't the true reason for two seders, it certainly comes in handy. But what about seder with friends?

Such problems the Jews fleeing Egypt didn't have to worry about, but we do. And the best way to deal with these potentially sticky situa-tions is to discuss them openly and consider alter-natives that meet your needs.

Some options: a) a third seder (oh, God!); b) rotate between one seder for family and one for friends; c) invite everybody together to the same seder or the synagogue seder; d) solve the problem by going away to one of the hotels that offer vacation plans for all of Passover week!

Selecting a Haggaddah

People will be coming to the seder from different experiences, so consider carefully the *Haggaddah* that you will use.

Selecting a Haggaddah that fits the needs of your household is a challenging task. They vary in tone, length, religious and political views, clarity of typeface, and graphics.

Some Haggaddahs provide side-by-side translation of the Hebrew text. Some even include transliteration of the Hebrew prayers into English letters, which is very helpful when including non-Hebrew readers.

Included here are several Haggaddahs that might appeal to you:

A Passover Hagadah. Editor, Rabbi Herbert Bronstein. New York: Central Rabbis (Reform), 1974. A nice contemporary selection of traditional prayers and thought-provoking readings illustrated to enhance the themes. Useful with varied ages. Plan your seder and figure out in advance which readings to include or skip.

Maxwell House Deluxe Edition Hagadah. Editor, Rabbi Bernard Levy. New York: General Foods Corporation, 1982. This Haggaddah is found in many homes . . . thanks to Maxwell House Coffee. It is a basic (Orthodox) Haggaddah with an archaic English translation. However, the price is right and it is useful.

The Animated Haggadah: A Text for Children. Rony Oren and Uri Shinar. Woodhaven, New York: Scopus Films, 1985. A delightful Haggaddah written for elementary-school readers illustrated by Rony Oren's claymation. Look for the accompanying activity book.

On the Wings of Freedom: The Hillel Hagadah for the Nights of Passover. Editor and translator, Rabbi Richard Levy. Hoboken, New Jersey: KTAV Publishing House, 1989. Good explanations, soulful Hebrew translations, gender-neutral language, spiritual sensitivity. Plan your seder, selecting prayer and reading alternatives that fit your guests.

The Passover Hagadah. Editor, Rachel Rabinowicz. New York: Rabbinical Assembly (Conservative), 1982. Dramatic, colorful illustrations. Good directions and explanations for the leader.

Gates of Freedom. Editor, Rabbi Chaim Stern. Bedford, New York: New Star Press, 1981. Good use of Hebrew transliterations alongside the Hebrew and English. Contemporary readings and interpretations; lovely illustrations. Useful with children.

A Family Hagadah. Editor, Shoshana Silverman. Rockville, Maryland: Kar-Ben Copies, Inc., 1987. A simple Haggaddah with clear discussion topics set side-by-side with the text. Great for seder leaders with clever ways to include many generations.

My Very Own Haggadah. Judyth Robbins Saypol. Rockville, Maryland: Kar-Ben Copies, Inc., 1974. A simple Haggaddah for early readers; children can color it in. Includes musical notations.

You can purchase Haggaddahs from bookstores throughout the country or through catalogues.

Planning the Seder Service

To make the seder meaningful, the leaders must take time to prepare. Although sometimes one person leads the seder, in many homes the responsibility is shared. Parts of the seder can be assigned ahead of time to encourage involvement by individuals or families. Guests might bring toys, drawings, or puppets to illustrate parts of the service.

Consideration of the starting time and length of the seder is important. How long can the children—or the adults—sit, talk, and discuss meaningfully until dinner is served? Plan the highlights of the seder accordingly.

Use the time the children are away from the table to enhance the adult discussions. All in all, each participant should feel included in the seder experience.

What time do you plan to end the seder? Plan to end dinner in time to do the concluding service. Focus on the highlights of the conclusion of the seder.

Seder Plate

The focus of the seder table is a seder plate, which holds the ritual foods. The seder plate can be an ordinary plate large enough to hold all the items, or it can be more elaborate, specially designed for the holiday. Some are made from ceramics, silver, copper, or brass. They often are decorated with images from the Passover story.

On the seder plate we place:

1. *Karpas*—a green leafy vegetable which is a reminder of springtime. People use parsley or any type of lettuce. Jews of Eastern European origin often use potatoes because their ancestors used potatoes (green vegetables were scarce!). We dip the karpas in salted water at the beginning of the service to remind us of the tears of slavery.

2. *Maror*—bitter herbs which remind us of the pain of slavery. Use either romaine lettuce or, for the hearty folk, use pieces of fresh horseradish. Cut some pieces ahead of time and place the horseradish root on the seder plate.

3. *Zeroah*—the roasted shankbone, symbol of the Passover sacrifice in the ancient Temple. Order from the butcher in advance. For the veggies, feel comfortable with a roasted beet or yam.

4. *Charoset*—a mixture of fruits, nuts, wine, and spices, which reminds us of the mortar that the Jews used to build Egyptian pyramids. Although various recipes abound, combinations of apples, nuts, and cinnamon, or cooked figs, pears, and apricots with cinnamon are most popular (see "**Recipes**").

5. *Betzah*—a roasted egg, symbol of the Passover sacrifice made at the ancient Temple in Jerusalem. Remember to hard-boil it first, then roast it in the oven, to prevent the "egg all over the oven" scene . . . an experience you do not want.

Matzah

Also found on the table is enough matzah for all. Commercially produced matzah is available in many supermarkets. Some people prefer *matzah shmurah,* round, hard, handmade matzah, which can be purchased at specialty stores.

The matzah is placed in a napkin or matzah cover specially made with three inside pockets. The middle matzah, the *afikoman,* is used as part of the conclusion of the seder. Afikoman means dessert in Greek and is the last food eaten during the seder. (See "**Activities**" for afikoman customs.)

Wine

Wine or grape juice is needed for the four cups of wine. Four cups of wine are specified in the service because four different verbs are found in the Haggaddah to describe being freed from bondage: "I am the Lord your God and I will *free* you . . . *deliver* you . . . *redeem* you . . . and *take* you . . . to be my people."

OF SWEET AND NOT-SO-SWEET WINE

At both our houses for Passover the variety of kosher for Passover wine on the table rivals a wine cellar. We don't stick only to the traditional sweet wine (no, this is not required for Passover), but have kosher wine varieties from California, France, Italy, Spain, Israel. Some of these wines are dry, some semidry, but there's something for everyone's palate.

A fun activity prior to Passover is a wine-tasting party. Invite friends and enjoy sampling the different varieties for your seder table.

Additional Ritual Items

Also placed on the table are a wine cup for Elijah the prophet, who, according to tradition, visits every home at Passover, candlesticks for the holiday, salt water for dipping, matzah covers, and afikoman bag. (See "Activities" to help you make some of these ritual items; buying them is not necessary.) Some people add pillows at every seat to represent the ancient custom in which free people reclined at a feast.

Searching for Hametz

On the night before the first seder many people search for hametz in their homes. Materials needed are a feather, a candle (or a flashlight for safety), and a plastic bag. One person hides pieces of bread throughout the house that were saved specifically for this purpose. Others then search by the candle's light for the last remains of the year's old harvest. Another person sweeps the area underneath the bread with the feather and scoops the hametz into a plastic bag.

As you begin the search, recite the following blessing: Blessed are You Adonai, Eternal One, Who allows us to prepare for Passover.

The next morning, you may gather the saved hametz and burn it in the backyard. Once everything is burned, recite the following: We have knowingly removed all hametz from our home and our hearts and are ready to experience Passover freedom.

THE SEDER

Most Haggaddahs will begin the seder, which literally means the service order, with the listing of its sections. Included here is an overview of the major sections:

1. *Halachma Anya*—This the Bread of Our Affliction: This section invites all who are hungry to come and eat alongside the Jewish people.

This can be accomplished prior to the holiday: Give all hametz—leavened foods—to a food pantry. Send a check to Sova, the Jewish food pantry in Los Angeles (Sova, JCCA, 5870 West Olympic Blvd., Los Angeles, CA 90036), or the national organization that feeds the poor or homeless, Mazon (Mazon: A Response to Jewish Hunger, 2940 Westwood Blvd., Suite 7, Los Angeles, CA 90064), or contribute to Oxfam America (115 Broadway, Boston, MA 02116). In addition, synagogues and Jewish federations have special appeals for funds to provide Passover food for the Jewish poor.

2. *Ma Nishtana*—Why Is This Night Different?: This is probably the most well-known section of the seder as children learn to sing it from an early age. This phrase begins the four questions that note the distinction between Passover and all other nights of the year. Usually the youngest child sings the questions.

These questions set the tone for the telling of the Passover story. Encourage discussion around these questions. In addition, what other questions might you ask? What additional aspects of the seder are not clear? Try to have young and old ask and answer the questions.

FAMOUS PASSOVER QUESTIONS, OR "WHO ATE THE BRISKET?"

As in all events that are planned for and anticipated in advance, Passover offers myriad possibilities for things to go wrong. But some Passover disasters create family stories that live on with a life of their own, to be enjoyed over and over again—after the shock of the incident.

The case of the missing brisket: Friends of ours cooked their kosher brisket early the day of the first seder. They left the brisket on top of the stove and went out shopping. When they returned, the entire brisket was gone. It had simply disappeared!

After a complete search of the house and yard, they found a tiny piece left near the doghouse. Their dog had eaten the entire brisket—and the kosher butchers were already closed for the holiday! Luckily they had helpful friends!

3. *Avadeem Hayeenu*—We Were Slaves to Pharoah in Egypt: This section illustrates that all of us, even today, would still be slaves in Egypt if the great Exodus had not occurred.

Each Jew can therefore reexperience the horror of slavery. No matter how successful, how influential, how intelligent, how rich, Jews are still obligated to tell and retell the story of the Exodus from Egypt. The retelling of that pivotal Jewish redemption empowers each person to pass on the gift of freedom to the next generation.

4. *Arba Banim*—The Four Children: Four different children with different interests and abilities are described in this section. Four types of children are highlighted to stress that all people must be taught, guided, and instructed in ways unique to that individual. Considering that the Haggaddah dates from approximately the second century, it is remarkable that the rabbis understood even then the need for individualized learning.

Learning is a personal experience, and learning about the Exodus can be shaped to meet the different social, educational, and emotional needs of each person. How can we use different teaching techniques in the seder? Act out parts of the service, use props, make poems, design a desert backdrop, or taste the foods.

5. *Arami Oved Avi*—My Father Was a Wandering Aramean: This section reveals the early history of the Jewish people and the reasons that they moved south into Egypt.

In the Haggaddah, below each paragraph of this text, are further interpretations. Look for a Haggaddah that treats this section in a way that is interesting to you. Enhance it with "actors" who appear in costume and dramatize their roles.

6. *Eser Makot*—The Ten Plagues: The plagues that were rained upon the Egyptians are recited. A drop of wine is removed from each cup at the mention of each plague. In this way Jews recognize the pain of their enemies, and their own joy is reduced because of the acknowledgment of other human suffering.

Some Haggaddahs add modern interpretations of plagues: What plagues do we experience today? Are they sent by God? What plagues must we rid ourselves of to experience a modern redemption?

We conclude this section with the singing of *Dayyanu,* the song that acknowledges that even one of God's great acts "would have been enough." In this song Jews express gratitude for all the acts that God performed for their survival.

7. *Rabban Gamliel Haya Omer*—Rabbi Gamliel Said: The central symbols of the seder are explained—the shankbone, the matzah, and the maror. The Haggaddah presents explanations of the symbols, but feel free to add your own interpretations.

8. *Bchol Dor V'dor*—In Every Generation: Each individual must see him/herself as having been personally redeemed by God through the exodus experience. This section points to the theological point of Passover—each Jew was liberated by God from Egyptian slavery. At that moment, each person experienced political liberation and spiritual freedom.

At the seder other liberations from a contemporary Egypt might be discussed: the experiences of Holocaust survivors and the liberation of Soviet, Iranian, and Ethiopian Jews.

PASSOVER AND THE WARSAW GHETTO UPRISING

Along with the exodus from Egypt, there is a modern-day liberation attempt that occurred at Passover. During Passover of 1943 the Jews of the Warsaw Ghetto, reduced to a tiny remnant and without food or supplies, rose up against armored German soldiers. For several days this tiny group stopped the nazi war machine. Although ultimately the uprising was crushed, the Jews demonstrated to the world their belief in liberation.

In "The Diary of Chaim Kaplan," the author, who did not survive the Warsaw Ghetto although his diary did, details the existence of the Jews during the years behind the walls of the ghetto. One of the most compelling comparisons is the difference in each successive Passover—from the first one, when the Jews had matzah and other Passover food, until the last, when without food and hope they rose up in one final challenge.

As we celebrate this holiday, may we truly appreciate the privilege to openly celebrate in freedom.

---

9. The concluding blessings of the seder praise God and stress the hope of future redemption for all people. Eat the afikoman, open the door for the Prophet Elijah, and conclude with the last glass of wine, saying, "Next year in Jerusalem."

The Last Days

The final day (or days) of Pesach is a full holiday; no work takes place and specific holiday prayers are added to the daily liturgy. Candles are lit with the onset of sundown, Passover *Kiddush* is recited, and the matzah blessed.

On the evening of the last day, *Yizkor* candles are lit for beloved relatives who are remembered.

SYNAGOGUE TRADITIONS

Morning Services

The synagogue customs for Passover are similar to those for Sukkot and Shavuot. We read specific Torah portions linked to the holiday theme and sing *Hallel*, the holiday psalms.

The intermediate days of the holiday are considered "half-holidays" in which we recite part of the Hallel psalms. On the Shabbat during Pesach, many congregations sing the ancient love poetry of Song of Songs, which highlights the love relationship between a man and a woman and, some say, also the love relationship between God and the Jewish people.

During the final Passover morning service in synagogue, the Yizkor service is recited. Jews remember both their personal loved ones and the martyrs of the Jewish people.

INSIGHTS

Names of the Holiday

Passover is best known as *Hag HaPesach*, referring to the biblical story in which God passed over the Jewish people while killing the Egyptian firstborn (Exodus 11:4–5; 12:23). This horrid tenth plague influenced Pharoah to free the Israelite people from their four-hundred-year bondage.

Passover is also known as *Hag Hamatzot*, the holiday in which Jews eat matzah, the unleavened bread.

Its additional name is *Hag HaAviv*, the springtime holiday, in which agricultural and spiritual signs of spring add to the festivities.

Freedom to Choose

With the benefit of freedom gained through the exodus, we now have the responsibility to choose. We choose to work, to rest, to worry, to celebrate, to believe. Consider the variety of choices we make as individuals, as members of groups, as families. What values support our choices for a rich spiritual life?

How can you gain strength as you continue to celebrate an ancient freedom holiday? What aspects of this holiday touch you and make you treasure freedom?

Redeeming Captives

Because the experience of slavery in Egypt is imprinted in the Jewish mind, the Jewish obligation to redeem captives became binding. Maimonides, a great medieval rabbi and scholar, clarified this obligation.

He noted that "redemption of captives takes precedence over supporting the poor or clothing them, for there is no greater deed. For the problems of the captive include the problems of the hungry, the thirsty, the naked, and the one in mortal danger" *(Mishneh Torah)*.

At Passover, Jews continue the redeeming process. Who now is in need of redemption? What can we do to free the contemporary captive?

Women: Shifrah and Puah

In Moses' time the midwives Shifrah and Puah are credited with resisting Pharoah's demand that all Jewish male babies be put to death. These women risked their own lives to save the infants. In actuality, two seemingly powerless women gained control through active resistance.

This historical example of women empowering themselves serves as a model to all of us to resist immoral orders by superiors. We can also learn, as did these women, to trust in ourselves and act on our beliefs.

ACTIVITIES

1. In preparation for Passover, you can make various art projects for your seder table. Materials like ceramics, papier-mâché, clear plastic cups, and so on can be used as a base for making seder plates, Elijah's cup, or other Kiddush cups.

For example, take an ordinary paper plate and paint it with tempura paints. After it is dry, paint with white glue to hold the colors and protect against moisture. Design the five places for the ritual items. Let dry. Use as your seder plate.

2. Matzah covers can be made by decorating plain cloth napkins or handkerchiefs. Use embroidery, cross stitching, or block printing to include Passover symbols or spring scenes on the matzah covers.

3. Unique family traditions can be centered around this holiday. Some families take photos of the seder table and guests before the beginning of the seder each year. These photos create an ongoing family history. You can use this opportunity to collect Passover stories from your guests, creating your own oral history project each year.

4. Some folks may want to experience their ancestral wandering in the desert. Consider camping, moving from Egypt to the Red Sea, as part of your Passover experience. You might do a simple seder in the desert and note the difference you feel from a seder at home.

5. Transitions from slavery to freedom can happen in our own lives. Take time during Passover to consider where you may have been entrapped in the last year and how you can free yourself. Perhaps the family has not had enough time together due to hectic schedules. Consider how you can each "free" up additional time to spend together. Are there other things you are carrying around as excess baggage? Consider how a "spring cleaning" can free your soul.

6. For the urbanites among us, take a trip to the country during the Passover week—notice spring's arrival and, for those in cold climates, experience the freedom of the warm weather.

7. Many songs are associated with the seder. Consider collecting a few musical tapes that will widen your musical repertoire for the holiday: Cindy Paley produced *A Singing Seder,* which is a helpful collection for seder preparation (write to her at: 14246 Chandler Blvd., Van Nuys, CA 91401). Classic recordings to look for are sung by Theodore Bikel, Richard Tucker, and Jan Peerce.

If musicians are members of your circle, encourage them to accompany or even highlight part of the seder through music.

8. If you find the array of Haggaddahs not tailor made for you, make your own loose-leaf family Haggaddah. Although the structure of the seder remains the same, the readings, poetry, songs, and discussions change over the years. Duplicate enough for the seder and enjoy!

You can also make a child's Haggaddah by folding several pieces of colored construction paper together. Punch holes in one side and tie ribbon to bind the booklet. Encourage children to imagine and re-create the various Haggaddah scenes, using felt pens, colored pencils, or crayons. Decorate the cover with a picture of "freedom." And don't forget to have the artist sign his/her work.

9. Today videos are available to help in the preparation for Pesach. A delightful and informative one is the *Animated Hagadah,* produced by Scopus Films, 150 Fifth Avenue, Suite 1102, New York, NY 10011, (212) 807-1020. Contact Jewish book stores and catalogues for more videos, as this is a growing field.

10. Books to supplement the Passover experience for children include: *But this Night Is Different: A Seder Experience* by A.F. Marcus and R. Zwerin (New York: Union of American Hebrew Congregations, 1980); *The Mouse in the Matzah Factory* by Francine Medoff (Rockville, Maryland: Kar-Ben Copies, Inc., 1983).

11. Afikoman charity: It is traditional for the child who finds the hidden afikoman to "demand" a reward to return the afikoman before the seder may be completed. In other households, all children receive an afikoman prize. We like this innovation: The child who finds the afikoman chooses a charity that the adults will contribute to after Pesach. This is a wonderful way for children to truly feel involved in the Passover *mitzvah* of "feeding the poor."

RECIPES

The cook's survival course through Pesach includes the abbreviation KISS: Keep It Short and Simple. Don't overdo—instant frozen foods are available. Consider some catering help if many people are attending the seder; fresh fruits and nuts make great desserts after the whole meal.

WHO SAYS MATZAH BALLS HAVE TO BE ROUND?

Passover can be a harrowing time for those who don't love to cook. The two of us often compare our memorable cooking disasters before each Passover.

Each year Phyllis makes at least two different attempts at matzah balls before they are edible. One year the matzah balls clouded the entire soup pot in one large mass. And her attempts at egg white cookies—well, the less said, the better.

And Karen's Passover desserts have also been known to go flatter than flat and to taste like nothing. Not to mention the time she substituted red pepper for black in her matzah balls.

Let's face it, this holiday is not about cooking, even if it sometimes seems so. It's about freedom—even freedom from the kitchen.

Sample Menu Plans

SEDER #1:
Wines and Seder Ritual Foods
Gefilte Fish with Horseradish
Chicken Soup with Matzah Balls
Roasted Chicken or Roast Beef
Potato Kugel
Broccoli
Fruits, Macaroons, and Nuts

SEDER #2:
Wines and Seder Ritual Foods
Fresh Vegetable-Dill Soup with
  Matzah Balls
Fresh Sole Wrapped Around Salmon
Asparagus
Roasted New Potatoes
Fruits, Macaroons, and Nuts

SENTA'S GERMAN MATZAH BALLS (THEY'RE SUPPOSED TO BE HEAVY!)

4 matzahs
2 Tbsp. unsalted margarine
1 whole egg (or 2 egg whites)
¼ small onion, chopped fine
1–2 tsp. chopped parsley

1 cup matzah meal, add more if needed
⅛ tsp. pepper
¼ tsp. ginger
⅛ tsp. nutmeg
1 tsp. salt, to taste

Crumble the matzahs and soak in warm water. Drain water and squeeze mixture as dry as possible. Melt margarine in frying pan; add onions and fry until golden.

Add matzah mixture, stir for a few minutes until warmed. Remove from heat. Add in eggs, spices, parsley. Mix thoroughly and let stand in refrigerator for ½ hour.

Remove from refrigerator and shape mixture into balls (the size of a quarter); roll balls in a little matzah meal to hold the shape. Put on paper plates and store flat. May be frozen if done ahead.

Before cooking, test one matzah ball by putting in boiling water or soup. If it separates, roll each matzah ball in a dusting of additional matzah meal. Cook in soup until the matzah balls rise to the top. Recipe makes 6–8 matzah balls.

NOTE: For those who want lighter matzah balls, use the recipe on the box of matzah meal or the kosher for Passover mix.

CHAROSET—THE "MORTAR"—THREE KINDS

ASHKENAZIC STYLE:
4–5 peeled and cored apples, grated
1 cup chopped almonds, pecans, or

walnuts
2 tsp. cinnamon
4–6 Tbsp. sweet red wine

Peel and grate apples. Add nuts and wine to bind. Stir. Ready to serve 5–6 people.

ISRAELI STYLE:
1 peeled and cored apple
3 sliced bananas
½ cup pitted and chopped dates
½ cup almonds

juice and rind of one orange
juice and rind of one lemon
½ cup dry red wine
1 tsp. cinnamon

Stir together. Add more nuts or even matzah meal if too thin. This serves 10–12 people.

SEPHARDIC STYLE:
1 pound pitted and chopped dates
½ cup apricots
½ cup figs
4 peeled and chopped apples
½ cup sweet red wine

1 tsp. cinnamon
¼ tsp. cloves
¼ nutmeg
1 cup chopped pecans (optional: can be
*   made without nuts for those with*
*   allergies)*

Peel and chop apples. Simmer with dried fruit. Cook until the apples are tender and the mixture is almost like jam. Cool and add the nuts. Serves 15 people.

PESACH BLESSINGS

Introductory meditation to be recited together before candle lighting:

Today we gather to thank God for all the goodness in our lives, for the beauty of nature, for the love we feel for one another, for the Pesach tradition which we share. May our celebration increase our awareness of your ongoing gifts, O God.

Candle lighting:
        (Recite this blessing, then light the candles on the first and last days. If it is Shabbat, light the candles first, then recite the blessing.)

Baruch Ata Adonai Elohaynu Melech Haolam, asher keedshanu b'mitzvotav v'tzivanu l'hadleek ner shel (Shabbat v') Yom Tov.
Blessed are You Adonai, Eternal One, Who enables us to welcome (Shabbat and) Pesach by kindling these lights.

Shehehayanu:
        (On the first night of Pesach add:)
Baruch Ata Adonai Elohaynu Melech Haolam, shehehayanu, v'keeyomanu v'higeeyanu laz'man hazeh.
Blessed are You Adonai, Eternal One, Who has kept us alive, sustained us, and encouraged us to celebrate this joyful festival.

Parents' blessing for their children:
        (Place hands on children and recite.)

FOR BOYS:
May God touch you as you strive to live in the image of Ephraim and Menasshe, leaders who carried on our traditions with pride.

FOR GIRLS:
May God touch you as you strive to live in the image of Sarah and Rebeccah, Rachel and Leah, leaders who carried on our traditions with pride.

CONTINUE SAYING FOR BOTH:
May the Eternal bless you and keep you.
May the Eternal bring you warmth and protect you.
May the Eternal embrace you and grant you peace. Amen.

Pesach Evening Kiddush to be used for the holiday nights and Shabbat:
    (Raise wine cups and recite. Then drink wine.)

We praise God with this symbol of fullness, and give thanks for the opportunities we have to share life's blessings.

Baruch Ata Adonai Elohaynu Melech Haolam, boray p'ree hagafen.
Blessed are You Adonai, Eternal One, Who creates fruit from the vine.

Baruch Ata Adonai Elohaynu Melech Haolam, asher bachar banu meekol ahm, v'romemanu meekol lashon, v'keedshanu b'meetzvotav. V'teetayn lanu, Adonai Elohaynu, b'ahavah (Shabbatot leemnucha oo) moadeem l'seemcha, chageem u'z-maneem l'sasson et yom (haShabbat hazeh v'et) yom hag hamatzot hazeh, z'man hayrutaynu, mikrah kodesh zaycher l'tzeeat meetzrayim. Kee banu bacharta v'otanu keedashta meekol ha-ahmeem, (v'Shabbat) oo'moaday kodshecha (b'ahavah oo'vrat-zon) b'seemcha oo'vsasson heenhaltanu). Baruch Ata Adonai, M'kadesh (ha-Shab-bat v') Yisrael, v'hazmaneem. Baruch Ata Adonai Elohaynu Melech Haolam, shehehayanu v'keeyomanu v'higeeyanu laz'man hazeh.

Blessed are You Adonai, Eternal One, Who has chosen us from among all people, sanctified us with holy acts, and given us times and seasons for rejoicing. (Shabbat and) Pesach remind us of the times for celebration, recalling the exodus from Egypt. You have distinguished us from all people, and have given us (the Shabbat and) holy festivals full of joy and inspiration. Blessed are You Adonai, Eternal One, Who sanctifies (the Shabbat,) the people Israel, and our sacred seasons.

Daytime Kiddush for holidays and Shabbat:
  (Raise wine cups and recite. Then drink the wine.)

El Moaday Adonai Meekrah-ay kodesh, asher teekrehoo otam b'moadam. VayDaber Moshe et moaday Adonai el b'nay Yisrael.
These are the sacred times appointed by God; and you shall announce them in their season.
Baruch Ata Adonai Elohaynu Melech Haolam, boray p'ree hagafen.
Blessed are You Adonai, Eternal One, Who creates the fruit from the vine.

Blessing over the matzah:
  (Remove matzah cover and recite. Then give each person a piece of matzah.)

Baruch Ata Adonai Elohaynu Melech Haolam, hamotzi lechem meen ha-aretz.
Blessed are You Adonai, Eternal One, Who creates matzah from the earth.

10
SHAVUOT—
ACCEPTANCE OF TORAH

SEVEN weeks after Passover the early summer holiday of Shavuot arrives. Its name literally means "weeks" and is a reminder of the link between these two pilgrimage harvest festivals.

The focus of Shavuot is the biblical story in which the Israelites wandered from Egypt through the desert to Mount Sinai, where they received the *Torah,* the Hebrew Bible. Each year Jews reexperience the giving of Torah at Mount Sinai and each year they reaccept that sacred tradition. Those born as Jews and those choosing to join the Jewish people through conversion affirm yearly their commitment to Judaism.

Shavuot is known as *Zman Matan Torataynu*—the season of the giving of the Torah (*Talmud* B. Shabbat 86b). It is also known as *Hag Hakatzir,* the harvest festival, which emphasizes the agricultural roots of this holiday as the harvest of the first spring crops.

Shavuot is celebrated for one day in Israel and by Reform synagogues; others in the Jewish community celebrate two days. All who are able should not work or attend school on these days.

GREETINGS

On Shavuot, friends and family greet each other with *"Hag Sameach*—Happy Holiday."

HOME TRADITIONS

Evening

Shavuot is welcomed at home by decorating with fresh flowers and spring plants. The table is set with a fine tablecloth, wine, and *challah.*

   As with Shabbat, the holiday begins at night with the reciting of the blessings and the lighting of two candles. This occurs with the setting of the sun, or the gathering for dinner, depending on one's customs. Following the candle lighting, it is traditional for parents to bless their children.

   On Shavuot, Jews recall their ancestors, and one *Yizkor* candle is lit in memory of each close relative who has died. (There is no blessing that accompanies the lighting of this special candle.)

   At the table, *Kiddush,* the prayer over the wine, is chanted, followed by the blessing of the *challah*. Jews recite the *Shehehayanu* prayer, acknowledging gratitude for reaching this season in life. *Birkat Hamazon,* the thanksgiving prayer, is recited at the conclusion of the meal.

Although Shavuot may feel like Shabbat, it is unique in its themes and its flavors. Most folks eat only dairy products for this holiday. This symbolizes that as Jews entered the promised land, they entered the land of "milk and honey."

Daytime

After morning services a festive dairy lunch is served. The ritual order is the same as the previous evening, starting with Kiddush. As on Shabbat, people socialize, relax, play games, or simply enjoy each other's company throughout the afternoons.

SYNAGOGUE TRADITIONS

Evening Service and Study

Many temples today have revived the ancient tradition of *Tikun Lel Shavuot,* a midnight-to-early-morning study session on the first night of Shavuot, concluding with an outdoor sunrise service. The topics discussed can range from the story of Ruth that focuses on intermariage and conversion to contemporary Israeli politics to ancient and modern Jewish poets. The evening is accompanied by sweets and coffee to fuel the participants through the wee hours.

Morning Services

Those who have studied and prayed throughout the night fall into bed before others have even thought of entering the synagogue for the holiday. However, the synagogue repeats the early-morning service for those who have opted for a night of sleep at home.

The synagogue customs for Shavuot are similar to the other two pilgrimage festivals, Pesach and Sukkot. Specific *Torah* portions linked to the holiday themes are read in the morning services. The congregation sings *Hallel,* which literally means praise, and is recited on joyous holidays. The Hallel prayer is composed of selections of poetry from Psalms 113 through 118.

The Torah portions for Shavuot highlight the experience of the giving of the Torah at Mount Sinai. On the first day the dramatic scene in which the Torah is given is read from Exodus 19–20, which includes the Ten Commandments. On the second day of the festival the laws regarding Temple practices are read from Deuteronomy 15:19–16:17. The additional text for Shavuot is the Book of Ruth.

Many Conservative, Reconstructionist, and Reform congregations celebrate the ceremony of Confirmation on Shavuot. At the conclusion of their formal religious education, teenagers publicly "confirm" their ongoing commitment to Judaism.

Yizkor, memorial prayers, are recited on Shavuot on either the first or second day. This is one of four times a year in which Yizkor is recited.

INSIGHTS

Torah: What Are Its Origins?

The Torah, which literally means a teaching, is the word used to indicate the whole of the Hebrew Bible. According to tradition, the Torah was given by God to the Jewish people. Due to this tradition, the Torah was believed to be the word of God.

Orthodox Judaism continues to view the Bible as the word of God given to Moses at Mount Sinai. This belief asserts that God created the text and therefore it is truth.

During the last two hundred years, as scholars have retrieved ancient documents and discovered clues to ancient languages, new views have developed regarding the origins of the Torah.

Scholars noted the influences of Egyptian, Babylonian, and other Near Eastern cultures on the biblical narrative. They noticed repetitions and variations of stories within the Bible that indicated possible human scribal errors or variations in authors. They noticed that other cultures and language groups had narratives paralleling the biblical stories, which indicated that portions of the text may have come from other peoples' traditions.

Many scholars began to acknowledge that the Torah may have developed from the daily experiences of the Jewish people. As such, it was a compiled text that captured the evolving experiences of the Jewish people with each other and other nations. Thus, the Torah defined Jewish values and beliefs and revealed the Jewish relationship with the Divine as seen from the human perspective.

This theory that acknowledges the various influences on the Bible is called the Documentary Hypothesis, developed primarily by Karl Graf and Julius Wellhausen in nineteenth-century Germany. It suggests that four major schools of thought developed different strands of sacred traditions which, when woven together by about the year 400 B.C.E., evolved into the single text known as the Torah.

Today the liberal Jewish movements—the Conservative, Reconstructionist and Reform—view the Torah as a document which was developed over centuries by human beings out of their encounters with each other and the Divine. This philosophy enables the liberal religious movements to interpret and change the traditions.

As you continue to study, you may find your views on the origins of Torah evolving. Good luck as you discover your own path.

Conversion

The Book of Ruth, read on Shavuot, provides a dramatic example of a woman fervently committed to a family, a way of life, and a belief. After her husband died, Ruth could have returned to the Moabites, her own people. Rather, Ruth chose freely to remain with her mother-in-law, Naomi, and become a member of the Jewish people. Ruth becomes a Jew as she proclaims: "Your people shall be my people, your

God my God, where you go I will go, where you will be buried, I will be buried" (Ruth 1:16–17).

Although through the centuries intermarriage has been perceived as a threat to the survival of the Jewish people, intermarriage is very much a reality today. Current statistics indicate that "one out of every three marriages of Jewish people will involve an intermarriage . . ." (Winer, M., "Sociological Research on Jewish Intermarriage," *Journal of Reform Judaism* (32) 1985, pp. 38–57).

The Jewish nation is small and every member of the community counts in terms of continuing and passing on an ancient and valued tradition. When Jews marry non-Jews and leave the Jewish community, the individual and the Jewish community both lose. The community grieves for the important link in the "family" of Judaism and the individual forfeits his/her historic and cultural bond to the Jewish people.

When intermarried couples decide to celebrate both religions, it can be quite stressful. Does religion become a power issue in the couple's relationship? What beliefs do they share and transmit to their children? The children of an intermarried couple will be fortunate if the parents can give the children a sense of belonging to one religion.

Conversion has been a formalized way into the Jewish faith for generations. Couples and individuals, like Ruth, choose to become members of the Jewish people through a step-by-step learning process that leads to a formal conversion ceremony.

Reasons for Conversion

Couples may want a common religious and cultural tradition within their homes. One partner may be willing to change his/her previous faith or explore a belief for the first time or may want to feel a connection to an ancient history and religious experience.

In other cases, one partner may be willing to convert to calm the fears the new in-laws express. At times, conversion can be seen as a step to premarital and marital conflict resolution. But conversion without personal commitment to Judaism may have limited effect in resolving marital conflict.

Conversion is a process that is slow and demands introspection. It can be meaningful if the conversion to Judaism is claimed by the newcomers as their own choice and not only an act that pleases others.

How to Convert

Individuals considering conversion should make an appointment with a rabbi to discuss the avenues open to them. Historically some rabbis would discourage potential converts by turning them away to ensure that the potential converts were convinced that Judaism was what they truly wanted.

Most rabbis do not do this today. However, they may encourage a series of discussions exploring motivation to convert, previous experience with Jews and Judaism, family life, and visions of what Judaism can bring to their lives.

"Introduction to Judaism" courses are offered for interested students and their partners. Most formal instruction includes study in Jewish customs and history, rituals, and home life. Many courses are supplemented by support groups that encourage a personal sharing of these experiences: What is it like to become Jewish? What do I lose in relation to my family of origin? What can I gain as I establish myself in a new family situation?

In addition, the student (or couple) meets with a sponsoring rabbi during the time of study. Here the student can explore theological, spiritual, and personal questions on a one-to-one basis.

Ceremony

Conversion is concluded with a ceremony that includes several steps. When completing the coursework, students may be asked to meet with a "court" of three rabbis. The rabbis will explore the students' learning and discuss their commitments to Jewish life.

After this, the students may go to a *mikveh,* a ritual bath, for the ritual immersion. At this time they are given a Hebrew name and are welcomed as Jews. Males may then proceed to a ritual circumcision.

And finally, a private or public ceremony will be held in the synagogue at which the convert is formally welcomed into the Jewish community.

The conversion process usually continues over a period of six to twelve months. However, feeling that one is Jewish may come in waves. Some converts feel they have experienced their lives as Jews since birth. Some feel that only after lighting Shabbat candles over a period of years does the religion and culture become "theirs." Some feel comfortable until faced with a trauma such as the death of a parent. Like other changes, this one is slow and gradual.

Each branch of Judaism places its stamp of welcome onto the convert in a slightly different manner. Reform, Reconstructionist, and Conservative rabbis usually accept each others' conversions. Usually, Orthodox rabbis accept only Orthodox conversions. The Conservative and Reform movements have formal programs to encourage ongoing discussion and support for these new members in their congregations. Don't hesitate to ask for some help. Contact the branches of Judaism or local temples to clarify the procedures in your community.

The stages of entering the Jewish people have changed some since the time of Ruth. But the process is there, and acceptance of new members into the Jewish world continues. Welcome aboard!

ACTIVITIES

1. Keep a diary as if you were Moses preparing to receive the Torah. What did you think as you climbed that mountain by yourself? What did you feel as the Torah was given? What did you experience as you walked down the mountain, carrying the Torah for all the Jewish people, for all time?

2. What was it like to be a Jew at the foot of Mount Sinai? Look at the biblical story and fill in between the lines. Produce a play that can let others experience that powerful event.

3. Make pictorial Torahs from cloth or parchment paper. Select plain material (muslin is a good choice) cut into several pieces that each measures 11″ × 17″.

Choose several stories that appeal to you and illustrate each story with crayon or cloth shapes onto a separate piece of cloth. Sew each section together with colored thread. Attach each end of the scroll to a 2′ stick. Roll the entire scroll the same as a Torah. Tie with a cloth ribbon.

4. You might enjoy meeting a calligrapher and learning about the ancient craft of writing and illustrating Jewish manuscripts. Or try it yourself.

5. Consider making Mount Sinai from clay or papier-mâché. Use toy figures and act out the dramatic giving of the Torah.

6. Examine the Ten Commandments. How do they apply to you? How can you make them work in the world? What other laws would you have included in these most central concerns?

7. Read the Book of Ruth. Notice the family interaction: Who cares for whom? Who leads the action? How is it accepted? Can you accept a new member into your family as easily as Naomi did? Can we learn from Naomi and from Ruth? How do you feel about someone choosing to enter the Jewish religion?

8. Spend Shavuot in the country. Go with a group of friends and make your own retreat. Study, cook, hike, and enjoy the leisure of Shavuot in the out-of-doors.

9. Create a Tikun Lel Shavuot at home with friends. Select a few sources of Jewish thought that you would like to read and discuss. Set the time, provide tea and desserts, and go into the night.

10. For the chefs, Shavuot provides the opportunity for the ultimate cheesecake bakeoff. When else can you mix calories and belief?

RECIPES

In the relaxing days of Shavuot, one can enjoy making blintzes and cheesecake. These caloric delights add to the holiday celebration.

Cheesecake recipes abound, so follow your own choice. Blintzes can be made or bought frozen.

Basic Blintzes

BATTER:
4 eggs, well beaten
1 tsp. salt
2 cups water
1½ cups flour

FILLING:
½ lb. cream cheese
2 lbs. farmer cheese
½ cup brown sugar
2 eggs
raisins, if desired

Beat eggs well; add salt and water. Gradually beat with rotary beater until smooth. Grease skillet with margarine. Pour out thin pancake; cook until pancake curls away from the edge of skillet. Cook on one side only. Remove from heat.

Add filling; fold like envelope. Return blintz to skillet and fry in margarine, fold side down, till slightly browned. Then turn and brown on other side. Blintzes can be wrapped with paper and frozen until ready to fry. Serve with sour cream, yogurt, jam, or fruit.

SHAVUOT BLESSINGS

Introductory meditation to be recited together prior to candle lighting:

In ancient times Jews celebrated this harvest festival by going up to Jerusalem. There they gathered at the Temple and offered fruit and grains in thanksgiving for the bounty of the natural world.

Today we gather to thank God for all the goodness in our lives, for the beauty of nature, for the love we feel for one another, for the Shavuot tradition which we share. May our celebration increase our awareness of your ongoing gifts, O God.

Candle lighting:

    (Recite this blessing, then light the candles on all nights but Shabbat evening. If it is Shabbat, light the candles first, then recite the blessing.)

Baruch Ata Adonai Elohaynu Melech Haolam, asher keedshanu b'mitzvotav v'tzivanu l'hadleek ner shel (Shabbat v') Yom Tov.

Blessed are You Adonai, Eternal One, Who enables us to welcome (Shabbat and) Shavuot by kindling these candles.

Shehehayanu:

    (On the first night of Shavuot add:)

Baruch Ata Adonai Elohaynu Melech Haolam, shehehayanu, v'keeyomanu v'higeeyanu laz'man hazeh.

Blessed are You Adonai, Eternal One, Who has kept us alive, sustained us, and encouraged us to celebrate this joyful festival.

Parents' blessing for their children:
    (Place hands on children and recite.)

FOR BOYS:
May God touch you as you strive to live in the image of Ephraim and Menasshe, leaders who carried on our traditions with pride.

FOR GIRLS:
May God touch you as you strive to live in the image of Sarah and Rebeccah, Rachel and Leah, leaders who carried on our traditions with pride.

CONTINUE SAYING FOR BOTH:
May the Eternal bless you and keep you.
May the Eternal bring you warmth and protect you.
May the Eternal embrace you and grant you peace. Amen.

Evening Kiddush:
    (Raise wine cups and recite. Then drink the wine.)

We praise God with this symbol of fullness, and give thanks for the opportunities we have to share life's blessings.

Baruch Ata Adonai Elohaynu Melech Haolam, boray p'ree hagafen.
Blessed are You Adonai, Eternal One, Who creates fruit from the vine.

Baruch Ata Adonai Elohaynu Melech Haolam, asher bachar banu meekol ahm, v'romemanu meekol lashon, v'keedshanu b'meetzvotav. V'teetayn lanu, Adonai Elohaynu, b'ahavah (Shabbatot leemnucha oo) moadeem l'seemcha, chageem u'z-maneem l'sasson et (haShabbat hazeh v'et) yom hag hashavuot zman matan Torah-taynu, mikrah kodesh zaycher l'tzeeat meetzrayim. Kee banu bacharta v'otanu keedashta meekol ha-ahmeem, (v'Shabbat) oo'moaday kodshecha (b'ahavah oo'vrat-zon) b'seemcha oo'vsasson heenhaltanu). Baruch Ata Adonai M'kadesh (ha-Shabbat v') Yisrael, v'hazmaneem.

Blessed are You Adonai, Eternal One, Who has chosen us from among all people, sanctified us with holy acts, and given us special times and seasons for rejoicing. (Shabbat and) Shavuot remind us of the times for celebration, recalling the gift of Torah from Mount Sinai. You have distinguished us from all people, and have given us (the Shabbat and) holy festivals full of joy and gladness. Blessed are You Adonai, Eternal One, Who sanctifies (the Shabbat,) the people Israel, and our sacred seasons.

Daytime Kiddush:
(Raise wine cups and recite. Then drink the wine.)

El Moaday Adonai Meekrah-ay kodesh, asher teekrehoo otam b'moadam. VayDaber Moshe et moaday Adonai el b'nay Yisrael.
These are the sacred times appointed by God; and you shall announce them in their season.
Baruch Ata Adonai Elohaynu Melech Haolam, boray p'ree hagafen.
Blessed are You Adonai, Eternal One, Who creates fruit from the vine.

Blessing over the challah:
(Remove challah cover and recite. Then give each person a piece of bread.)

Baruch Ata Adonai Elohaynu Melech Haolam, hamotzi lechem meen ha-aretz.
Blessed are You Adonai, Eternal One, Who creates bread from the earth.

APPENDIX

1. The Jewish Calendar—A Different Cycle

The Jewish calendar is based on aspects of the solar and lunar calendars, which are different from the secular calendar based primarily on the solar calendar.

The beginnings and endings of each Jewish month are determined by the appearance and disappearance of the moon. Yet the beginning of each Jewish year is dependent on the earth's position in relationship to the sun. The confluence of those two cycles form the Jewish calendar.

In early times determinations regarding the beginning of each month were made by witnessed accounts of the actual sighting of the new moon. Approximately 400, Rabbi Hillel II is credited with having developed a mathematical formula to scientifically determine the beginning of each month. This system was later changed only slightly, and for the last one thousand years Jews have used the same calendar.

Usually the Jewish year is made up of 354 days, which is composed of 12 months of 29 or 30 days. Adjustments are made to keep months in their appropriate season by adding a 13th month every two or three years. In a 19-year cycle there are seven years that contain the 13th month, called *Adar Sheni,* the Second Adar.

Although the Jewish dates of the holidays do not change in the Jewish calendar, the dates of the Jewish holidays vary in the secular calendar. As an example, Rosh Hashanah always occurs in the fall season but varies from early September to mid-October. Because of this variation it is necessary to consult a Jewish calendar for each holiday's secular date.

For your convenience, here is a list of holidays and their corresponding secular dates through the year 2005. Each Jewish year begins with Rosh Hashanah and overlaps parts of two secular years. For example, the Jewish year 5753 begins in the fall of 1992 and overlaps the end of 1992 and the beginning of 1993.

Jewish holidays begin in the evening and are listed here as such:

5753 (1992–93)

Rosh Hashanah begins Sunday night September 27, 1992
Yom Kippur begins Tuesday night October 6, 1992
Sukkot begins Sunday night October 11, 1992
Shmini Atzeret begins Sunday night October 18, 1992
Simchat Torah begins Monday night October 19, 1992
Hanukkah begins Saturday night December 19, 1992
Tu B'Shvat begins Friday night, February 5, 1993
Purim begins Saturday night March 6, 1993
Passover begins Monday night April 5, 1993
Shavuot begins Tuesday night May 25, 1993
Tisha B'Av begins Monday night July 26, 1993

5754 (1993–94)

Rosh Hashanah begins Wednesday night September 15, 1993
Yom Kippur begins Friday night September 24, 1993
Sukkot begins Wednesday night September 29, 1993
Shmini Atzeret begins Wednesday night October 6, 1993
Simchat Torah begins Thursday night October 7, 1993
Hanukkah begins Wednesday night December 8, 1993
Tu B'Shvat begins Wednesday night January 26, 1994
Purim begins Thursday night February 24, 1994
Passover begins Saturday night March 26, 1994
Shavuot begins Sunday night May 15, 1994
Tisha B'Av begins Saturday night July 16, 1994

5755 (1994–95)

Rosh Hashanah begins Monday night September 5, 1994
Yom Kippur begins Wednesday night September 14, 1994
Sukkot begins Monday night September 19, 1994
Shmini Atzeret begins Monday night September 26, 1994
Simchat Torah begins Tuesday night September 27, 1994
Hanukkah begins Sunday night November 27, 1994

Tu B'Shvat begins Sunday night January 15, 1995
Purim begins Wednesday night March 15, 1995
Passover begins Friday night April 14, 1995
Shavuot begins Saturday night June 3, 1995
Tisha B'Av begins Saturday night August 5, 1995

5756 (1995–96)

Rosh Hashanah begins Sunday night September 24, 1995
Yom Kippur begins Tuesday night October 3, 1995
Sukkot begins Sunday night October 8, 1995
Shmini Atzeret begins Sunday night October 15, 1995
Simchat Torah begins Monday night October 16, 1995
Hanukkah begins Sunday night December 17, 1995
Tu B'Shvat begins Sunday night February 4, 1996
Purim begins Monday night March 4, 1996
Passover begins Wednesday night April 3, 1996
Shavuot begins Thursday night May 23, 1996
Tisha B'Av begins Wednesday night July 24, 1996

5757 (1996–97)

Rosh Hashanah begins Friday night September 13, 1996
Yom Kippur begins Sunday night September 22, 1996
Sukkot begins Friday night September 27, 1996
Shmini Atzeret begins Friday night October 4, 1996
Simchat Torah begins Saturday night October 5, 1996
Hanukkah begins Thursday night December 5, 1996
Tu B'Shvat begins Wednesday night January 22, 1997
Purim begins Saturday night March 22, 1997
Passover begins Monday night April 21, 1997
Shavuot begins Tuesday night June 10, 1997
Tisha B'Av begins Monday night August 11, 1997

5758 (1997–98)

Rosh Hashanah begins Wednesday night October 1, 1997
Yom Kippur begins Friday night October 10, 1997
Sukkot begins Wednesday night October 15, 1997
Shmini Atzeret begins Wednesday night October 22, 1997
Simchat Torah begins Thursday night October 23, 1997

Hanukkah begins Tuesday night December 23, 1997
Tu B'Shvat begins Tuesday night February 10, 1998
Purim begins Wednesday night March 11, 1998
Passover begins Friday night April 10, 1998
Shavuot begins Saturday night May 30, 1998
Tisha B'Av begins Saturday night August 1, 1998

5759 (1998–99)

Rosh Hashanah begins Sunday night September 20, 1998
Yom Kippur begins Tuesday night September 29, 1998
Sukkot begins Sunday night October 4, 1998
Shmini Atzeret begins Sunday night October 11, 1998
Simchat Torah begins Monday night October 12, 1998
Hanukkah begins Sunday night December 13, 1998
Tu B'Shvat begins Sunday night January 31, 1999
Purim begins Monday night March 1, 1999
Passover begins Wednesday night March 31, 1999
Shavuot begins Thursday night May 20, 1999
Tisha B'Av begins Wednesday night July 21, 1999

5760 (1999–2000)

Rosh Hashanah begins Friday night September 10, 1999
Yom Kippur begins Sunday night September 19, 1999
Sukkot begins Friday night September 24, 1999
Shmini Atzeret begins Friday night October 1, 1999
Simchat Torah begins Saturday night October 2, 1999
Hanukkah begins Friday night December 3, 1999
Tu B'Shvat begins Friday night January 21, 2000
Purim begins Monday night March 20, 2000
Passover begins Wednesday night April 19, 2000
Shavuot begins Thursday night June 8, 2000
Tisha B'Av begins Wednesday night August 9, 2000

5761 (2000–01)

Rosh Hashanah begins Friday night September 29, 2000
Yom Kippur begins Sunday night October 8, 2000
Sukkot begins Friday night October 13, 2000
Shmini Atzeret begins Friday night October 20, 2000

Simchat Torah begins Saturday night October 21, 2000
Hanukkah begins Thursday night December 21, 2000
Tu B'Shvat begins Wednesday night February 7, 2001
Purim begins Thursday night March 8, 2001
Passover begins Saturday night April 7, 2001
Shavuot begins Sunday night May 27, 2001
Tisha B'Av begins Saturday night July 28, 2001

5762 (2001–02)

Rosh Hashanah begins Monday night September 17, 2001
Yom Kippur begins Wednesday night September 26, 2001
Sukkot begins Monday night October 1, 2001
Shmini Atzeret begins Monday night October 8, 2001
Simchat Torah begins Tuesday night October 9, 2001
Hanukkah begins Sunday night December 9, 2001
Tu B'Shvat begins Sunday night January 27, 2002
Purim begins Monday night February 25, 2002
Passover begins Wednesday night March 27, 2002
Shavuot begins Thursday night May 16, 2002
Tisha B'Av begins Wednesday night July 17, 2002

5763 (2002–03)

Rosh Hashanah begins Friday night September 6, 2002
Yom Kippur begins Sunday night September 15, 2002
Sukkot begins Friday night September 20, 2002
Shmini Atzeret begins Friday night September 27, 2002
Simchat Torah begins Saturday night September 28, 2002
Hanukkah begins Friday night November 29, 2002
Tu B'Shvat begins Friday night January 17, 2003
Purim begins Monday night March 17, 2003
Passover begins Wednesday night April 16, 2003
Shavuot begins Thursday night June 5, 2003
Tisha B'Av begins Wednesday night August 6, 2003

5764 (2003–04)

Rosh Hashanah begins Friday night September 26, 2003
Yom Kippur begins Sunday night October 5, 2003
Sukkot begins Friday night October 10, 2003

Shmini Atzeret begins Friday night October 17, 2003
Simchat Torah begins Saturday night October 18, 2003
Hanukkah begins Friday night December 19, 2003
Tu B'Shvat begins Friday night February 6, 2004
Purim begins Saturday night March 6, 2004
Passover begins Monday night April 5, 2004
Shavuot begins Tuesday night May 25, 2004
Tisha B'Av begins Monday night July 26, 2004

5765 (2004–05)

Rosh Hashanah begins Wednesday night September 15, 2004
Yom Kippur begins Friday night September 24, 2004
Sukkot begins Wednesday night September 29, 2004
Shmini Atzeret begins Wednesday night October 6, 2004
Simchat Torah begins Thursday night October 7, 2004
Hanukkah begins Tuesday night December 7, 2004
Tu B'Shvat begins Monday night January 24, 2005
Purim begins Thursday night March 24, 2005
Passover begins Saturday night April 23, 2005
Shavuot begins Sunday night June 12, 2005
Tisha B'Av begins Saturday night August 13, 2005

2. Additional Holidays—The Minor Ones

Several minor holidays have not thus far been described in this book. These include:

a. Rosh Hodesh—First day of each Jewish month; sometimes celebrated as a women's holiday.

b. Lag B'Omer—33rd day of the counting of the days between Passover and Shavuot; sometimes celebrated as a picnic day.

c. Tisha B'Av—9th of Av; a fast day in July or August; the destructions of Jerusalem are remembered.

d. Yom HaShoah—Holocaust Remembrance Day, marked shortly after Passover; those who were murdered under the nazi regime are remembered.

e. Yom HaAtzmaut—Israeli Independence Day celebrated on May 14; the importance of the State of Israel is emphasized.

3. Referral List

Many times throughout this book the different movements within Judaism are referred to. Listed below are the national offices for these movements and, in addition, two national Jewish organizations:

Conservative:
United Synagogue of America
155 Fifth Avenue
New York, NY 10010
212-533-7800

Orthodox:
Union of Orthodox Congregations
333 Seventh Avenue
New York, NY 10001
212-563-4000

Reform:
Union of American Hebrew Congregations
838 Fifth Avenue
New York, NY 10021
212-249-0100

Reconstructionist:
Reconstructionist Rabbinical College
Church Road and Greenwood Avenue
Wyncote, PA 19095
215-576-0800

Council of Jewish Federations
730 Broadway
New York, NY 10003
212-598-3500

Jewish Community Centers Associations
15 East 26th Street
New York, NY 10010
212-532-4949

INDEX

ABOUT THE ILLUSTRATOR

VICKI REIKES FOX is the founding director of the Museum of the Southern Jewish Experience near Jackson, Mississippi. She is also an artist specializing in illuminated manuscripts, Jewish wedding contracts, and ceremonial art. She is working on an illustrated children's book. She lives with her family in Los Angeles, California.